The Fortunes of Captain Blood

The Fortunes of
Captain Blood

By

RAFAEL SABATINI

The American Reprint Company

NEW YORK

Published 1976 by Special Arrangement

Library of Congress Catalog Card Number 81-71969
International Standard Book Number 0-89190-743-2

To Order, Contact:
AMERICAN REPRINT COMPANY
Box 1200
Mattituck, New York 11952

Manufactured in the United States of America

Contents

✦❧✦

The Dragon's Jaw

SHE WAS A beautiful ship, in the frigate class, fashioned, not merely in her lines but in her details, with an extreme of that loving care that Spanish builders not infrequently bestowed. She had been named, as if to blend piety with loyalty, the *San Felipe,* and she had been equipped with a fastidiousness to match the beauty of her lines.

The great cabin, flooded with sunlight from the tall stern windows of horn, which now stood open above the creaming wake, had been made luxurious by richly carved furnishings, by hangings of green damask and by the gilded scrollwork of the bulkheads. Here Peter Blood, her present owner, bending over the Spaniard, who reclined on a daybed by the stern locker, was reverting for the moment to his original trade of surgery. His hands, as strong as they were shapely, and by deftness rendered as delicate of touch as a woman's, had renewed the dressing of the Spaniard's thigh, where the fractured bone had pierced the flesh. He made now a final adjustment of the strappings that held the splint in place, stood up, and by a nod dismissed the Negro steward who had been his acolyte.

'It is very well, Don Ilario.' He spoke quietly in a Spanish that was fluent and even graceful. 'I can now give you my word that you will walk on your two legs again.'

A wan smile dispelled some of the shadows from the hollows which suffering had dug in the patient's patrician countenance.

'For that,' he said, 'the thanks to God and you. A miracle,' he said.

'No miracle at all. Just surgery.'

'Ah! But the surgeon, then? That is the miracle. Will men believe me when I say I was made whole again by Captain Blood?'

Peter Blood, tall and lithe, was in the act of rolling down the sleeves of his fine cambric shirt. His eyes, so startlingly blue under their black eyebrows, in that hawk-face tanned to the colour of mahogany, gravely considered his guest.

'Once a surgeon, always a surgeon,' he said, as if by way of explanation. 'And I was a surgeon once, as you may have heard.'

'As I have discovered for myself, to my profit. But by what queer alchemy of Fate does a surgeon become a buccaneer?'

Captain Blood smiled reflectively.

'My troubles came upon me from considering only—as in your case—a surgeon's duty; from beholding in a wounded man a patient, without concern for how he came by his wounds. He was a poor rebel who had been out with the Duke of Monmouth. Who comforts a rebel is himself a rebel. So runs the law among Christian men. I was taken red-handed in the abominable act of dressing his wounds, and for that I was sentenced to death. The penalty was commuted, not from mercy. Slaves were needed in the plantations. With a shipload of other wretches, I was carried overseas to be sold in Barbados. I escaped, and I think I must have died at somewhere about the time that Captain Blood came to life. But the ghost of the surgeon still walks in the body of the buccaneer, as you have found, Don Ilario.'

'To my great profit and deep gratitude. And the ghost still practises the dangerous charity that slew the surgeon?'

'Ah!' The vivid eyes flashed him a searching look, observed the flush on the Spaniard's pallid cheek-bones, the queer expression of his glance.

'You are not afraid that history may repeat itself?'

'I do not care to be afraid of anything,' said Captain Blood, and he reached for his coat. He adjusted to his shoulders the black satin garment rich with silver lace, adjusted before a mirror the costly Mechlin at his throat, shook out the curls of his black periwig, and stood forth, an elegant incarnation of virility, more proper to the antechambers of the Escurial than to the quarter-deck of a buccaneer ship.

'You must rest now and endeavour to sleep until eight bells is made. You show no sign of fever. But tranquillity is still my prescription for you.'

The patient, however, showed no disposition to be tranquil.

'Don Pedro . . . Before you go . . . Wait. This situation puts me to shame. I cannot lie so under this great obligation to you. I sail under false colours.'

Blood's shaven lips had an ironic twist.

'I have, myself, found it convenient at times.'

'Ah, but how different! My honour revolts.' Abruptly, his dark eyes steadily meeting the Captain's, he continued: 'You know me only as one of four shipwrecked Spaniards you rescued from that rock of the Saint Vincent Keys and have generously undertaken to land at San Domingo. Honour insists that you should know more.'

Blood seemed mildly amused.

'I doubt if you could add much to my knowledge. You are Don Ilario de Saavedra, the King of Spain's new Governor of Hispaniola. Before the gale that wrecked you, your ship formed part of the squadron of the Marquis of Riconete, who is to co-operate with you in the Caribbean in the extermination of that endemonized pirate and buccaneer, that enemy of God and Spain whose name is Peter Blood.'

Don Ilario's blank face betrayed the depth of his astonishment.

'*Virgen Santisima*—Virgin Most Holy! You know that?'

'With commendable prudence you put your commission in your pocket when your ship was about to founder. With a prudence no less commendable, I took a look at it soon after you came aboard. We are not fastidious in my trade.'

If the simple explanation removed one astonishment, it replaced it by another.

'And in spite of that, you not only use me tenderly; you actually convey me to San Domingo!' Then his expression changed. 'Ah, I see. You trust my gratitude, and . . .'

But there Captain Blood interrupted him.

'Gratitude?' He laughed. 'It is the last emotion in which I should put my trust. I trust to nothing but myself, sir. I have told you that I do not care to be afraid of anything. Your obligation is not to the buccaneer; it is to the surgeon; and that is an obligation to a ghost. So dismiss it. Do not trouble your mind with problems of where your duty lies: whether to me or to your king. I am forewarned. That is enough for me. Give yourself peace, Don Ilario.'

He departed, leaving the Spaniard bewildered and bemused.

Coming out into the waist, where some two score of his buccaneers, the half of the ship's full company, were idling, he detected a sullenness in the air, which earlier had been fresh and clear. There had, however, been no steadiness in the weather since the hurricane some ten days ago, on the morrow of which he had rescued the injured Don Ilario and his three companions from the rocky islet on which the storm had cast them up. It was due to these contrary winds of some violence, with intermittent breathless calms, that the *San Felipe* was still no nearer to her destination than a point some twenty miles south of Saona. She was barely crawling now over a gently heaving oily sea of deepest violet, her sails alternately swelling and sagging. The distant highlands of Hispaniola on the starboard quarter, which earlier had been clearly visible, had vanished now behind an ashen haze.

Chaffinch, the sailing master, standing by the whipstaff at the break of the poop, spoke to him as he passed.

'There's more mischief coming, Captain. I begin to doubt if we'll ever make San Domingo. We've a Jonah aboard.'

So far as the mischief went, Chaffinch was not mistaken. It came on to blow from the west at noon, and brought up such a storm that his lightly expressed doubt of ever making San Domingo came before midnight to be seriously entertained by every man aboard. Under a deluge of rain, to the crash of thunder, and with great seas pounding over her, the *San Felipe* rode out a gale that bore her steadily northwestward. Not until daybreak did the last of the hurricane sweep past her, leaving her, dipping and heaving on a black sea of long smooth rollers, to cast up her damage and lick her wounds. Her poop-rail had been shorn away, and her swivel-guns had gone with it overboard. From the boom amidships one of her boats had been carried off, and some parts of the wreckage of another lay tangled in the forechains. But of all that she had suffered above deck the most serious damage was to her mainmast. It had been sprung, and was not merely useless, but a source of danger. Against all this, however, they could set it that the storm had all but swept them to their destination. Less than five miles ahead, to the north, stood El Rosario, beyond which lay San Domingo. Into the Spanish waters of that harbour and under the guns of King Philip's fortresses, Don Ilario, for his own sake, must supply them with safe-conduct.

It was still early morning, brilliant now and sparkling after the tempest, when the battered ship, with mizzen and foresails ballooning to the light airs, but not a rag on her mainmast save the banner of Castile at its summit, staggered past the natural breakwater, which the floods of the Ozama have long since eroded, and came by the narrow eastern passage that was known as the Dragon's Jaw into the harbour of San Domingo.

She found eight fathoms close alongside of a shore that was reared like a mole on a foundation of coral forming an island then a quarter of a mile in width by nearly a mile in length, with a shallow ridge along the middle of it crowned by some clusters of cabbage-palms. Here the *San Felipe* dropped anchor and fired a gun to salute the noblest city of New Spain across the spacious harbour.

White and fair that city stood in its emerald setting of wide savannahs, a place of squares and palaces and churches that might have been transported from Castile, dominated by the spire of the cathedral that held the ashes of Columbus.

There was a stir along the white mole, and soon a string of boats came speeding towards the *San Felipe,* led by a gilded barge of twenty oars, trailing the red-and-yellow flag of Spain. Under a red awning fringed with gold sat a portly, swarthy, blue-jowled gentleman in pale brown taffetas and a broad plumed hat, who wheezed and sweated when presently he climbed the accommodation-ladder to the waist of the *San Felipe.*

There Captain Blood, in black-and-silver splendour, stood to receive him beside the day-bed on which the helpless Don Ilario had been carried from the cabin. In attendance upon him stood three shipwrecked companions, and for background there was a file of buccaneers, tricked out in headpieces and corselets to look like Spanish infantry, standing with ordered muskets.

But Don Clemente Pedroso, the retiring Governor, whom Don Ilario came to replace, was not deceived. A year ago, off Puerto Rico, on the deck of a galleon that Captain Blood had boarded and sacked, Pedroso had stood face to face with the buccaneer, and Blood's was not a face that was easily forgotten. Don Clemente checked abruptly in his advance. Into his swarthy, pear-shaped countenance came a blend of fear and fury.

Urbanely, plumed hat in hand, the Captain bowed to him.

'Yours excellency's memory honours me, I think. But do not suppose that I fly false colours.' He pointed aloft to the flag which had earned the *San Felipe* the civility of this visit. 'That is due to the presence aboard of Don Ilario de Saavedra, King Philip's new Governor of Hispaniola.'

Don Clemente lowered his eyes to the pallid proud face of the man on the day-bed, and stood speechless, breathing noisily, whilst Don Ilario in a few words explained the situation and proffered a commission still legible if sadly blurred by sea-water. The three Spaniards who had been rescued with him were also presented, and there was assurance that all further confirmation would be supplied by the Marquis of Riconete, the Admiral of the Ocean-Sea, whose squadron should very soon be at San Domingo.

In a scowling silence Don Clemente listened; in scowling silence he scanned the new Governor's commission. Thereafter he strove, from prudence, to wrap in a cold dignity the rage which the situation and the sight of Captain Blood aroused in him.

But he was in obvious haste to depart. 'My barge, Don Ilario, is at your excellency's orders. There is, I think, nothing to detain us.'

And he half-turned away, scorning in his tremendous dignity further to notice Captain Blood.

'Nothing,' said Don Ilario, 'beyond expressions of gratitude to my preserver and provision for his requital.'

Don Clemente, without turning, answered sourly:

'Naturally, I suppose, it becomes necessary to permit him a free withdrawal.'

'I should be shamed by so poor and stingy an acknowledgment,' said Don Ilario, 'especially in the present condition of his ship. It is a poor enough return for the great service he has rendered me to permit him to supply himself here with wood and water and fresh victuals and with boats to replace those which he has lost. He must be accorded sanctuary at San Domingo to carry out repairs.'

Captain Blood interposed.

'For those repairs I need not be troubling San Domingo. The island here will excellently serve, and, by your leave, Don Clemente, I shall temporarily take possession of it.'

Don Clemente, who had stood fuming during Don Ilario's announcement, swung about now and exploded.

'By my leave?' he cried, his face yellow. 'I render thanks to God and His Saints that I am relieved of that shame since Don Ilario is now the Governor.'

Saavedra frowned. He spoke with languid sternness. 'You will bear that in your memory, if you please, Don Clemente, and trim your tone to it.'

'Oh, your excellency's servant.' The deposed Governor bowed in raging irony. 'It is, of course, yours to command how long this enemy of God and of Spain shall enjoy the hospitality and protection of His Catholic Majesty.'

'For as long as he may need so as to carry out his repairs.'

'I see. And once these are effected, he is, of course, to be free to depart, so that he may continue to harass and plunder the ships of Spain?'

Frostily Saavedra answered.

'He has my word that he shall be free to go, and that for forty-eight hours thereafter there shall be no pursuit or other measure against him.'

'And he has your word for that? By all the Hells! He has your word . . .'

Blandly Captain Blood cut in.

'And it occurs to me that it would be prudent to have your word as well, my friend.'

He was moved by no fear for himself, but only by generosity to Don Ilario: to link the old Governor and the new in responsibility, so that Don Clemente might not hereafter make for his successor the mischief of which Blood perceived him capable.

Don Clemente was aghast. Furiously he waved his fat hands.

'My word! My word!' He choked with rage. His countenance swelled as if it would burst. 'You think I'll pass my word to a pirate rogue? You think . . .'

'Oh, as you please. If you prefer it I can put you under hatches and in irons, and keep both you and Don Ilario aboard until I am ready to sail again.'

'It's an outrage.'

Captain Blood shrugged.

'You may call it that. I call it holding hostages.'

Don Clemente glared at him with increasing malice.

'I must protest. Under constraint . . .'

'There's no constraint at all. You'll give me your word, or I'll put you in irons. Ye've a free choice. Where's the constraint?'

Then Don Ilario cut in.

'Come, sir, come! This wrangling is monstrously ungracious. You'll pledge your word, sir, or take the consequences.'

And so, for all his bitterness, Don Clemente suffered the reluctant pledge to be wrung from him.

After that, in contrast with his furious departure was Don Ilario's gracious leave-taking when they were about to lower his day-bed in slings to the waiting barge. He and Captain Blood parted with mutual compliments and expressions of good-will, which it was perfectly understood should nowise hinder the active hostility imposed by duty upon Don Ilario once the armistice were at an end.

Blood smiled as he watched the red barge with its trailing flag ploughing with flash of oars across the harbour towards the mole. Some of the lesser boats went with it. Others, laden with fruit and vegetables, fresh meat and fish, remained on the flank of the *San Felipe,* little caring, in their anxiety to trade their wares, that she might be a pirate.

Wolverstone, the one-eyed giant who had shared Blood's escape from Barbados and had since been one of his closest associates, leaned beside him on the bulwarks.

'Ye'll not be trusting overmuch, I hope, to the word of that flabby, blue-faced Governor?'

'It's hateful, so it is, to be by nature suspicious, Ned. Hasn't he pledged himself, and would ye do him the wrong to suspect his bona fides? I cry shame on you, Ned; but all the same we'll be removing temptation from him by fortifying ourselves on the island here.'

They set about it at once, with the swift, expert activity of their kind. Gangways were constructed, con-

necting the ship with the island, and on that strip of sand
and coral they landed the twenty-four guns of the *San
Felipe,* and so emplaced them that they commanded the
harbour. They erected a tent of sail-cloth, felling palms
to supply the poles, set up a forge, and having un-
stepped the damaged mast, hauled it ashore so that they
might repair it there. Meanwhile, the carpenters aboard
set about making good the damage to the upper works,
whilst parties of buccaneers in the three boats supplied
to them by the orders of Don Ilario went to procure
wood and water and the necessary stores, for all of
which Captain Blood scrupulously paid.

For two days they laboured without disturbance or
distraction. When on the morning of the third day the
alarm came, it was not from the harbour or the town
before them, but from the open sea at their backs.

Captain Blood was fetched ashore at sunrise, so that
from the summit of the ridge he might survey the approaching peril. With him went Wolverstone and Chaffinch, Hagthorpe, the West Country gentleman who
shared their fortunes, and Ogle, who once had been a
gunner in the King's Navy.

Less than a mile away they beheld a squadron of five
tall ships approaching in a bravery of ensigns and pennants, all canvas spread to the light but quickening
morning airs. Even as they gazed, a white cloud of
smoke blossomed like a cauliflower on the flank of the
leading galleon, and the boom of a saluting gun came to
arouse a city that as yet was barely stirring.

'A lovely sight,' said Chaffinch.

'For a poet or a shipmaster,' said Blood. 'But I'm
neither of those this morning. I'm thinking this will be
King Philip's Admiral of the Ocean-Sea, the Marquis of
Riconete.'

'And he's pledged no word not to molest us,' was
Wolverstone's grim and unnecessary reminder.

'But I'll see to it that he does before we let him
through the Dragon's Jaw.'

Blood turned on his heel, and making a trumpet of his
hands, sounded his orders sharp and clearly to some

two or three score buccaneers who stood also at gaze, some way behind them, by the guns.

Instantly those hands were seething to obey, and for the next five minutes all was a bustle of heaving and hauling to drag the *San Felipe's* two stern-chasers to the summit of the ridge. They were demi-cannon, with a range of fully a mile and a half, and they were no sooner in position than Ogle was laying one of them. At a word from Blood he touched off the gun, and sent a thirty-pound shot athwart the bow of the advancing Admiral's ship, three quarters of a mile away.

There is no signal to lie hove-to that will command a more prompt compliance. Whatever the Marquis of Riconete's astonishment at this thunderbolt from a clear sky, it brought him up with a round turn. The helm was put over hard, and the ship swung to larboard with idly flapping sails. Faintly over the sunlit waters came the sound of a trumpet, and the four ships that followed executed the same manoeuvre. Then from the Admiral's flagship a boat was lowered, and came speeding towards the reef to investigate this portent.

Peter Blood, with Chaffinch and a half-score men, was at the water's edge when the boat grounded. Wolverstone and Hagthorpe had taken station on the other side of the island, so as to watch the harbour and the mole, which was now all agog.

An elegant young officer stepped ashore to request on the Admiral's behalf an explanation of the sinister greeting he had received. It was supplied.

'I am here refitting my ship by permission of Don Ilario de Saavedra, in return for some small service I had the honour to do him when he was lately shipwrecked. Before I can suffer the Admiral of the Ocean-Sea to enter this harbour, I must possess his confirmation of Don Ilario's sanction and his pledge that he will leave me in peace to complete my repairs.'

The young officer stiffened with indignation.

'These are extraordinary words, sir. Who are you?'

'My name is Blood. Captain Blood, at your service.'

'Captain . . . Captain Blood!' The young man's eyes

were round. 'You are Captain Blood?' Suddenly he laughed. 'You have the effrontery to suppose ...'

He was interrupted.

'I do not like "effrontery." And as for what I suppose, be good enough to come with me. It will save argument.' He led the way to the summit of the ridge, the Spaniard sullenly following. There he paused. 'You were about to tell me, of course, that I had better be making my soul, because the guns of your squadron will blow me off this island. Be pleased to observe.'

He pointed with his long ebony cane to the activity below, where a motley buccaneer host was swarming about the landed cannon. Six of the guns were being hauled into a new position so as completely to command at point-blank range the narrow channel of the Dragon's Jaw. On the seaward side, whence it might be assailed, this battery was fully protected by the ridge.

'You will understand the purpose of these measures,' said Captain Blood. 'And you may have heard that my gunnery is of exceptional excellence. Even if it were not, I might without boasting assert, and you, I am sure, are of intelligence to perceive that the first ship to thrust her bow-sprit across that line will be sunk before she can bring a gun to bear.' He leaned upon his tall cane, the embodiment of suavity. 'Inform your Admiral, with my service, of what you have seen, and assure him from me that he may enter the harbour of San Domingo the moment he has given me the pledge I ask; but not a moment sooner.' He waved a hand in dismissal. 'God be with you, sir. Chaffinch, escort the gentleman to his boat.'

In his anger the Spaniard failed to do justice to so courteous an occasion. He muttered some Spanish mixture of theology and bawdiness, and flung away in a pet, without farewells. Back to the Admiral he was rowed. But either he did not report accurately or else the Admiral was of those who will not be convinced. For an hour later the ridge was being ploughed by round shot, and the morning air shaken by the thunder of the squadron's guns. It distressed the gulls and set them circling and screaming overhead. But it distressed the buccaneers not at all, sheltered behind the natural bastion of the ridge from that storm of iron.

During a slackening of the fire, Ogle wriggled snake-wise up to the demi-cannons which had been so emplaced that they thrust up their muzzles and no more above the ridge. He laid one of them with slow care. The Spaniards, formed in line ahead for the purposes of their bombardment, three quarters of a mile away, offered a target that could hardly be missed. Ogle touched off the unsuspected gun and a thirty-pound shot crashed amidships into the bulwarks of the middle galleon. It went to warn the Marquis that he was not to be allowed to practise his gunnery with impunity.

There was a blare of trumpets and a hasty going-about of the entire squadron to beat up against the freshening wind. To speed them, Ogle fired the second gun, and although lethally the shot was harmless, morally it could scarcely fail of its alarming purpose. Then he whistled up his gun-crew to reload at leisure in that moment of the enemy's fleeing panic.

All day the Spaniards hove-to a mile and a half away, where they accounted themselves out of range. Blood took advantage of this to order six more guns to be hauled to the ridge, and so as to form a breastwork half the palms on the island were felled. Whilst the main body of the buccaneers, clothed only in loose leather breeches, made short work of this, the remainder under the orders of the carpenter calmly pursued the labours of refitting. The fire glowed in the forge, and the anvils pealed bell-like under the hammers.

Across the harbour and into this scene of heroic activity came towards evening Don Clemente Pedroso, greatly daring and more yellow-faced than ever. Conducted to the ridge, where Captain Blood with the help of Ogle was still directing the construction of the breastwork, his excellency demanded furiously to know what the buccaneers supposed must be the end of this farce.

'If you think you're propounding a problem,' said Captain Blood, 'ye're mistook. It'll end when the

Admiral gives me the pledge I've asked that he'll not molest me.'

Don Clemente's black eyes were malevolent, and malevolent was the crease at the base of his beaky nose.

'You do not know the Marquis of Riconete.'

'What's more to the matter is that the Marquis does not know me. But I think we shall soon be better acquainted.'

'You deceive yourself. The Admiral is bound by no promise made you by Don Ilario. He will never make terms with you.'

Captain Blood laughed in his face.

'In that case, faith, he can stay where he is until he reaches the bottom of his water-casks. Then he can either die of thirst or sail away to find water. Indeed, we may not have to wait so long. You've not observed perhaps that the wind is freshening from the south. If it should come to blow in earnest, your Marquis may be in some discomfort off this coast.'

Don Clemente wasted some energy in vague blasphemies. Captain Blood was amused.

'I know how you suffer. You were already counting upon seeing me hanged.'

'Few things in this life would bring me greater satisfaction.'

'Alas! I must hope to disappoint your excellency. You'll stay to sup aboard with me?'

'Sir, I do not sup with pirates.'

'Then you may go sup with the Devil,' said Captain Blood.

And on his short fat legs Don Clemente stalked in dudgeon back to his barge.

Wolverstone watched his departure with a brooding eye.

'Odslife, Peter, you'ld be wise to hold that Spanish gentleman. His pledge binds him no more than would a cobweb. The treacherous dog will spare nothing to do us a mischief, pledge or no pledge.'

'You're forgetting Don Ilario.'

'I'm thinking Don Clemente may forget him, too.'

'We'll be vigilant,' Blood promised confidently.

That night the buccaneers slept as usual in their quarters aboard, but they left a gun-crew ashore and set a watch in a boat anchored in the Dragon's Jaw, lest the Admiral of Ocean-Sea should attempt to creep in. But although the night was clear, other risks apart, the Spaniards would not attempt the hazardous channel in the dark.

Throughout the next day, which was Sunday, the condition of stalemate continued. But on Monday morning the exasperated Admiral once more plastered the island with shot, and then stood boldly in to force a passage.

Ogle's battery had suffered no damage because the Admiral knew neither its position nor extent. Nor did Ogle now disclose it until the enemy was within a half-mile. Then four of his guns blazed at the leading ship. Two shots went wide, a third smashed into her tall forecastle, and the fourth caught her between wind and water and opened a breach through which the sea poured into her. The other three Spaniards veered in haste to starboard, and went off on an easterly tack. The crippled, listed galleon went staggering after them, jettisoning in desperate haste her guns and what other heavy gear she could spare, so as to bring the wound in her flank above the water-level.

Thus ended that attempt to force a way in, and by noon the Spaniards had gone about again and were back in their old position a mile and a half away. They were still there twenty-four hours later when a boat went out from San Domingo with a letter from Don Ilario in which the new Governor required the Marquis of Riconete to accord Captain Blood the terms he demanded. The boat had to struggle against a rising sea, for it was coming on to blow again, and from the south dark ominous banks of cloud were rolling up. Apprehensions on the score of the weather may well have combined with Don Ilario's letter in persuading the

Marquis to yield where obstinacy seemed to promise only humiliation.

So the officer by whom Captain Blood had already been visited came again to the island at the harbour's mouth, bringing him the required letter of undertaking from the Admiral, as a result of which the Spanish ships were that evening allowed to come into shelter from the rising storm. Unmolested they sailed through the Dragon's Jaw, and went to drop anchor across the harbour, by the town.

The wounds in the pride of the Marquis of Riconete were raw, and at the Governor's Palace that night there was a discussion of some heat. It beat to and fro between the dangerous doctrine expounded by the Admiral and supported by Don Clemente that an undertaking obtained by threats was not in honour binding, and the firm insistence of the chivalrous Don Ilario that the terms must be kept.

Wolverstone's mistrust of the operation of the Spanish conscience continued unabated, and nourished his contempt of Blood's faith in the word that had been pledged. Nor would he account sufficient the measures taken in emplacing the guns anew, so that all but six still left to command the Dragon's Jaw were now trained upon the harbour. His single eye remained apprehensively watchful in the three or four peaceful days that followed, but it was not until the morning of Friday, by when, the mast repaired, they were almost ready to put to sea, that he observed anything that he could account significant. What he observed then led him to call Captain Blood to the poop of the *San Felipe*.

'There's a queer coming and going of boats over yonder, between the Spanish squadron and the mole. Ye can see it for yourself. And it's been going on this half-hour and more. The boats go fully laden to the mole, and come back empty to the ships. Maybe ye'll guess the reasoning of it.'

'The meaning's plain enough,' said Blood. 'The crews are being put ashore.'

'It's what I was supposing,' said Wolverstone. 'But

will you tell me what sense or purpose can there be in that? Where there's no sense there's usually mischief. There'ld be no harm in having the men stand to their arms on the island tonight.'

The cloud on Blood's brow showed that his lieutenant had succeeded in stirring his suspicions.

'It's plaguily odd, so it is. And yet . . . Faith, I'll not believe Don Ilario would play me false.'

'I'm not thinking of Don Ilario, but of that bile-laden curmudgeon Don Clemente. That's not the man to let a pledged word thwart his spite. And if this Riconete is such another, as well he may be . . .'

'Don Ilario is the man in authority now.'

'Maybe. But he's crippled by a broken leg, and those other two might easily overbear him, knowing that King Philip himself would condone it.'

'But if they mean mischief, why should they be putting the crews ashore?'

'That's what I hoped you might guess, Peter.'

'Since I can't, I'd better go and find out.' A fruit barge had just come alongside. Captain Blood leaned over the rail. 'Hey, you!' he hailed the owner. 'Bring me your yams aboard.'

He turned to beckon some of the hands in the waist and issued orders briefly whilst the fruit-seller was climbing the accommodation-ladder with a basket of yams balanced on his head. He was invited aft to the Captain's cabin, and unsuspecting went, after which he was seen no more that day. His half-caste mate, who had remained in the barge, was similarly lured aboard, and went to join his master under hatches. Then an unclean, barelegged, sunburned fellow in the greasy shirt, loose calico breeches and swathed head of a waterside hawker, went over the side of the *San Felipe* climbed down into the barge, and pulled away across the harbour towards the Spanish ships, followed by anxious eyes from the bulwarks of the buccaneer vessel.

Bumping alongside of the Admiral, the hawker bawled his wares for some time in vain. The utter silence within those wooden walls was significant. After a while steps rang out on the deck. A sentry in a headpiece looked over the rail to bid him take his fruit to the devil, adding the indiscreet but already superfluous information that if he were not a fool he would know that there was no one aboard.

Bawling ribaldries in return, the hawker pulled away for the mole, climbed out of the barge, and went to refresh himself at a wayside tavern that was thronged with Spaniards from the ships. Over a pot of wine he insinuated himself into a group of these seamen, with an odd tale of wrongs suffered at the hands of pirates and a fiercely rancorous criticism of the Admiral for suffering the buccaneers to remain on the island at the harbour's mouth instead of blowing them to perdition.

His fluent Spanish admitted no suspicion. His truculence and obvious hatred of pirates won him sympathy.

'It's not the Admiral,' a petty officer assured him. 'He'ld never have parleyed with these dogs. It's this weak-kneed new Governor of Hispaniola who's to blame. It's he who has given them leave to repair their ship.'

'If I were an Admiral of Castile,' said the hawker, 'I vow to the Virgin I'ld take matters into my own hands.'

There was a general laugh, and a corpulent Spaniard clapped him on the back.

'The Admiral's of the same mind, my lad.'

'In spite of his flabbiness the Governor,' said a second.

'That's why we're all ashore,' nodded a third.

And now in scraps which the hawker was left to piece together forth came the tale of mischief that was preparing for the buccaneers.

So much to his liking did the hawker find the Spaniards and so much to their liking did they find him that the afternoon was well advanced before he rolled out of the tavern to find his barge and resume his trade. The pursuit of it took him back across the harbour, and when at last he came alongside the *San Felipe* he was seen to have a second and very roomy barge in tow. Making fast at the foot of the accommodation-ladder he climbed to the ship's waist, where Wolverstone received him with relief and not without wrath.

'Ye said naught of going ashore, Peter? Where the plague was the need o' that? You'll be thrusting your head into a noose once too often.'

Captain Blood laughed.

'I've thrust my head into no noose at all. And if I had, the result would have been worth the risk. I'm justified of my faith in Don Ilario. It's only because he's a man of his word that we may all avoid having our throats cut this night. For if he had given his consent to employ the men of the garrison, as Don Clemente wished, we should never have known anything about it until too late. Because he refused, Don Clemente has made alliance with that other forsworn scoundrel, the Admiral. Between them they've concocted a sweet plan behind Don Ilario's back. And that's why the Marquis has taken his crews ashore so as to hold them in readiness for the job. They're to slip out to sea in boatloads at midnight by the shallow western passage, land on the unguarded southwest side of the island, and then, having entered by the back door as it were, creep across to surprise us on board the *San Felipe* and cut our throats while we sleep. There'll be some four hundred of them at the least. Practically every mother's son from the squadron. The Marquis of Riconete means to make sure that the odds are in his favour.'

'And we with eighty men in all!' Wolverstone rolled his single eye. 'But we're forewarned. We can shift the guns so as to smash them as they land.'

Blood shook his head.

'It can't be done without being noticed. If they saw us move the guns, they must suppose we've got wind of what's coming. They'ld change their plans, and that wouldn't suit me at all.'

'Wouldn't suit you! Does this *camisado* suit you?'

'Let me see the trap that's set for me, and it's odd if I can't turn it against the trapper. Did ye notice that I brought a second barge back with me? Forty men can pack into those two bottoms, the remainder can go in the four boats we have.'

'Go? Go where? D'ye mean to run, Peter?'

'To be sure I do. But no farther than will suit my purpose.'

He cut things fine. It wanted only an hour to midnight when he embarked his men. And even then he was in no haste to set out. He waited until the silence of the night was disturbed by a distant creak of rowlocks, which warned him that the Spaniards were well upon their way to the shallow passage on the western side of the island. Then, at last, he gave the word to push off, and the *San Felipe* was abandoned to the enemy stealing upon her through the night.

It would be fully an hour later, when the Spaniards, having landed, came like shadows over the ridge, some to take possession of the guns, others to charge across the gangways. They preserved a ghostly silence until they were aboard the *San Felipe*. Then they gave tongue loudly, as stormers will, to encourage themselves. To their surprise, however, not all the din they made sufficed to arouse these pirate dogs, who, apparently, were all asleep so trustfully that they had set no watch.

A sense of something outside their calculations began to pervade them as they stood at fault, unable to understand this lack of life aboard the ship they had invaded. Then, suddenly, the darkness of the harbour was split by tongues of flame from across the harbour, and with a roar as of thunder a broadside of twenty guns crashed its metal into the flank of the *San Felipe*.

The surprise party, thus itself surprised, filled the night with a screaming babel of imprecations, and turned in frenzy to escape from a vessel that was beginning to founder. In the mad panic of men assailed by forces of destruction which they cannot understand, the Spaniards fought one another to reach the gangways and regain the comparative safety of the shore without thought or care for those who had been wounded by that murderous volley.

The Marquis of Riconete, a tall, gaunt man, strove furiously to rally them.

'Stand firm! In the name of God, stand firm, you dogs!'

His officers plunged this way and that into the fleeing mob, and with blows and oaths succeeded in restoring some measure of order. Whilst the *San Felipe* was settling down in eight fathoms, the men, ashore and reformed at last, stood to their arms, waiting. But they no more knew for what they waited than did the Marquis, who was furiously demanding of Heaven and Hell the explanation of happenings so unaccountable.

It was soon afforded. Against the blackness of the night loomed ahead, in deeper blackness, the shape of a great ship that was slowly advancing towards the Dragon's Jaw. The splash of oars and the grating of rowlocks told that she was being warped out of the harbour, and to the straining ears of the Spaniards the creak of blocks and the rattle of spars presently bore the message that she was hoisting sail.

To the Marquis, peering with Don Clemente through the gloom, the riddle was solved. Whilst he had been leading the men of his squadron to seize a ship that he supposed to be full of buccaneers, the buccaneers had stolen across the harbour to take possession of a ship that they knew to be untenanted, and to turn her guns upon the Spaniards in the *San Felipe*. It was in that same vessel, the Admiral's flagship, the magnificent *Maria Gloriosa* of forty guns, with a fortune in her hold, that those accursed pirates were now putting to sea under the Admiral's impotent nose. He said so in bitterness, and in bitterness raged awhile with Don Clemente, until the latter suddenly remembered the guns that Blood had trained upon the passage, guns that would still be emplaced and of a certainty loaded, since they had not been used. Frantically he informed the Admiral of how he might yet turn the tables on the buccaneers, and at the information the Admiral instantly took fire.

'I vow to Heaven,' he cried, 'that those dogs shall

not leave San Domingo, though I have to sink my own ship. Ho, there! The guns! To the guns!'

He led the way at a run, half a hundred men stumbling after him in the dark towards the channel battery. They reached it just as the *Maria Gloriosa* was entering the Dragon's Jaw. In less than five minutes she would be within point-blank range. A miss would be impossible at such close quarters, and six guns stood ready trained.

'A gunner!' bawled the Marquis. 'At once a gunner, to sink me that infernal pirate into Hell.'

A man stood briskly forward. From the rear came a gleam of light, and a lantern was passed forward from hand to hand until it reached the gunner. He snatched it, ignited from its flames a length of fuse, then stepped to the nearest gun.

'Wait,' the Marquis ordered. 'Wait until she is abreast.'

But by the light of the lantern the gunner perceived at once that waiting could avail them nothing. With an imprecation he sprang to the next gun, shed light upon the touch-hole, and again passed on. Thus from gun to gun he sped until he had reached the last one. Then he came back, swinging the lantern in one hand and the spluttering fuse in the other, so slowly that the Marquis was moved to frenzy.

Not a hundred yards away the *Maria Gloriosa* was slowly passing, her hull a dark shadow, her sails faintly grey above.

'Make haste, fool! Make haste! Touch them off!' roared the Admiral of the Ocean-Sea.

'Look for yourself, excellency.' The gunner set down the lantern on the gun so that its light fell directly upon the touch-hole. 'Spiked. A soft nail has been rammed home. It is the same with all of them.'

The Admiral of the Ocean-Sea swore with the picturesque and horrible fervour that only a Spaniard can achieve. 'He forgets nothing, that endemonized pirate dog.'

A musket-shot, carefully aimed by a buccaneer from

the bulwarks of the passing ship, came to shatter the lantern. It was followed by an ironic cheer and a burst of still more ironic laughter from the deck of the *Maria Gloriosa* as she passed on her stately way through the Dragon's Jaw to the open sea.

The Pretender

1

MOBILITY, AS EVERYONE knows, is a quality that has been in all times a conspicuous factor of success with most great commanders by land and sea. So, too, with Captain Blood. There were occasions when his onslaught was sudden as the stoop of a hawk. And there was a time, coinciding with his attainment of the summit of his fame, when this mobility assumed proportions conveying such an impression of ubiquity that it led the Spaniards to believe and assert that only a compact with Satan could enable a man so miraculously to annihilate space.

Not content to be mildly amused by the echoes that reached him from time to time of the supernatural powers with which Spanish superstition endowed him, Captain Blood was diligent to profit where possible by the additional terror in which his name came thus to be held. But when shortly after his capture at San Domingo of the *Maria Gloriosa,* the powerful, richly laden flagship of the Spanish Admiral of the Ocean-Sea, the Marquis of Riconete, he heard it positively and circumstantially reported that on the very morrow of his sailing from San Domingo he had been raiding Cartagena, two hundred miles away, it occurred to him that one or two other fantastic tales of his doings that had lately reached his ears might possess a foundation less vague than was supplied by mere superstitious imaginings.

It was in a waterside tavern at Christianstadt on the Island of Sainte-Croix, where the *Maria Gloriosa* (impu-

dently renamed the *Andalusian Lass,* and as impudently flying the flag of the Union) had put in for wood and
water, that he overheard an account of horrors prac-
tised by himself and his buccaneers at Cartagena in the
course of that same raid.

He had sought the tavern in accordance with his usual
custom when roving at a venture, without definite object. These resorts of seafaring men were of all places
the likeliest in which to pick up scraps of information
that might be turned to account. Nor was this the first
time that the information he picked up concerned himself, though never yet had it been of quite so surprising
a nature.

The narrator was a big Dutchman, red of hair and
face, named Claus, master of a merchant ship from the
Scheldt, and he was entertaining with his lurid tale of
outrage two traders of the town, members of the French
West India Company.

Uninvited, Blood thrust himself into this group with
the object of learning more, and the intrusion was not
merely accepted with the tolerance that prevailed in
such resorts, but welcomed by virtue of the elegance of
this stranger's appointments and the quiet authority of
his manner.

'My greetings, messieurs.' If his French had not the
native fluency of his Spanish, acquired during two years
at Seville in a prison of the Holy Office, yet it was ser-
viceably smooth. He drew up a stool, sat down without
ceremony, and rapped with his knuckles on the stained
deal table to summon the taverner. 'When do you say
that this occurred?'

'Ten days ago it was,' the Dutchman answered him.

'Impossible.' Blood shook his periwigged head. 'To
my certain knowledge, Captain Blood ten days ago was
at San Domingo. Besides, his ways are hardly as vil-
lainous as those you describe.'

Claus, that rough man, of a temper to match his fiery
complexion, displayed impatience of the contradiction.

'Pirates are pirates, and all are foul.' He spat ostentatiously upon the sanded floor, as if to mark his nausea.

'Faith, I'll not argue with you on that. But since I know that ten days ago Captain Blood was at San Domingo, it follows that he could not at the same time have been at Cartagena.'

'Cocksure, are you not?' the Dutchman sneered. 'Then let me tell you, sir, that I had the tale two days since at San Juan de Puerto Rico from the captain of one of two battered Spanish plate ships that had been beset in Cartagena by the raiders. You'll not pretend to know better than he. Those two galleons ran into San Juan for shelter. They had been hunted across the Caribbean by that damned buccaneer, and they would never have escaped him but that a lucky shot of theirs damaged his foremast and compelled him to shorten sail.'

But Blood was not impressed by this citation of an eye-witness.

'Bah!' said he. 'The Spaniards were in a mistake. That's all.'

The traders looked uneasily at the dark face of this newcomer, whose eyes, so vividly blue under their black eyebrows, were coldly contemptuous. The timely arrival of the taverner brought a pause to the discussion, and Blood softened the mounting irritation of the Dutchman by inviting these habitual rum-drinkers to share with him a bottle of more elegant Canary sack.

'My good sir,' Claus insisted, 'there could be no mistake. Blood's big red ship, the *Arabella,* is not to be mistaken.'

'If they say that the *Arabella* chased them, they make it the more certain that they lied. For, again to my certain knowledge, the *Arabella* is at Tortuga, careened for graving and refitting.'

'You know a deal,' said the Dutchman with his heavy sarcasm.

'I keep myself informed,' was the plausible answer, civilly delivered. 'It's prudent.'

'Aye, provided that you inform yourself correctly. This time you're sorely at fault. Believe me, sir, at present Captain Blood is somewhere hereabouts.'

Captain Blood smiled.

'That I can well believe. What I don't perceive is why you should suppose it.'

The Dutchman thumped the table with his great fist.

'Didn't I tell you that somewhere off Puerto Rico his foremast was strained, in action with these Spaniards? What better reason than that? He'll have run to one of these islands for repairs. That's certain.'

'What's much more certain is that your Spaniards, in panic of Captain Blood, see an *Arabella* in every ship they sight.'

Only the coming of the sack made the Dutchman tolerant of such obstinacy in error. When they had drunk, he confined his talk to the plate ships. Not only were they at Puerto Rico for repairs, but after their late experience, and because they were very richly laden, they would not again put to sea until they could be convoyed.

Now here, at last, was matter of such interest to Captain Blood that he was not concerned to dispute further about the horrors imputed to him at Cartagena and the other falsehood of his engagement with those same plate ships.

That evening in the cabin of the *Andalusian Lass,* in whose splendid equipment of damasks and velvets, of carved and gilded bulkheads, of crystal and silver, was reflected the opulence of the Spanish Admiral to whom she had so lately belonged, Captain Blood summoned a council of war. It was composed of the one-eyed giant Wolverstone, of Nathaniel Hagthorpe, that pleasant-mannered West Country gentleman, and of Chaffinch, the little sailing master, all of them men who had been transported with Blood for their share in the Monmouth rising. As a result of their deliberations, the *Andalusian Lass* weighed anchor that same night, and slipped away from Sainte-Croix, to appear two days later off San Juan de Puerto Rico.

Flying now the red-and-gold of Spain at her main-truck, she hove-to in the roads, fired a gun in salute, and lowered a boat.

Through his telescope Blood scanned the harbour for confirmation of the Dutchman's tale. There he made out quite clearly among the lesser shipping two tall yellow galleons, vessels of thirty guns, whose upper works bore signs of extensive damage, now in course of repair. So far, then, it seemed, Mynheer Claus had told the truth. And this was all that mattered.

It was necessary to proceed with caution. Not only was the harbour protected by a considerable fort, with a garrison which no doubt would be kept more than usually alert in view of the presence of the treasure-ships, but Blood disposed of no more than eighty hands aboard the *Andalusian Lass,* so that he was not in sufficient strength to effect a landing, even if his gunnery should have the good fortune to subdue the fortress. He must trust to guile rather than to strength and in the lowered cockboat Captain Blood went audaciously ashore upon a reconnaissance.

2

It was so improbable as to be accounted impossible that news of Captain Blood's capture of the Spanish flagship at San Domingo could already have reached Puerto Rico; therefore the white and gold splendours and the pronouncedly Spanish lines of the *Maria Gloriosa* should be his sufficient credentials at the outset. He had made free with the Marquis of Riconete's extensive wardrobe, and he came arrayed in a suit of violet taffetas, with stockings of lilac silk and a baldrick of finest Cordovan of the same colour that was stiff with silver bullion. A broad black hat with a trailing claret feather covered his black periwig and shaded his weathered high-bred face.

Tall, straight, and vigorously spare, his head high, and authority in every line of him, he came to stand, leaning upon his tall gold-headed cane, before the Captain-General of Puerto Rico, Don Sebastian Mendes, and to explain himself in that fluent Castilian so painfully acquired.

Some Spaniards, making a literal translation of his name, spoke of him as Don Pedro Sangre, others alluded to him as El Diablo Encarnado. Humorously blending now the two he impudent announced himself as Don Pedro Encarnado, deputy of the Admiral of the Ocean-Sea, the Marquis of Riconete, who could not come ashore in person because chained to his bed aboard by an attack of gout. From a Dutch vessel, spoken off Sainte-Croix, his excellency the Admiral had heard of an attack by scoundrelly buccaneers upon two ships of Spain from Cartagena, which had sought shelter here at San Juan. These ships he had seen in the harbour, but the Marquis desired more precise information in the matter.

Don Sebastian supplied it tempestuously. He was a big, choleric man, flabby and sallow, with little black moustaches surmounting lips as thick almost as an African's and he possessed a number of chins, all of them blue from the razor.

His reception of the false Don Pedro had been marked, first by all the ceremony due to the deputy of a representative of the Catholic King, and then by the cordiality proper from one Castilian gentleman to another; he presented him to his dainty, timid, still youthful little wife, and kept him to dinner, which was spread in a cool, white patio under the green shade of a trellis of vines, and served by liveried Negro slaves at the orders of a severely formal Spanish majordomo.

At table the tempestuousness aroused in Don Sebastian by his visitor's questions was maintained. It was true enough—*por Dios!*—that the plate ships had been set upon by buccaneers, the same vile *hijos de puta* who had lately transformed Cartagena into the likeness of Hell. There were nauseating details, which the Captain-General supplied without regard for the feelings of Doña Leocadia, who shuddered and crossed herself more than once while his horrible tale was telling.

If it shocked Captain Blood to learn that such things

were being imputed to him and his followers, he forgot this in the interest aroused in him by the information that there was bullion aboard those plate ships to the value of two hundred thousand pieces of eight, to say nothing of pepper and spices worth almost the like amount.

'What a prize would not that have been for that incarnate devil Blood, and what a mercy of the Lord it was that the ships were able not only to get away from Cartagena, but to escape his subsequent pursuit of them!'

'Captain Blood?' said the visitor. 'Is it certain, then, that this was his work?'

'Not a doubt of it. Who else is afloat today who would dare so much? Let me lay hands on him, and as Heaven hears me I'll have the skin off his bones to make myself a pair of breeches.'

'Sebastian, my love!' Doña Leocadia shudderingly remonstrated. 'What horror!'

'Let me lay hands on him,' Don Sebastian fiercely repeated.

Captain Blood smiled amiably.

'It may come to pass. He may be nearer to you than you suppose.'

'I pray God he may be.' And the Captain-General twirled his absurd moustache.

After dinner the visitor took a ceremonious leave, regretfully, but of necessity since he must report to his Admiral. But on the morrow he was back again, and when the boat that brought him ashore had returned to the white and gold flagship, the great galleon was observed by the idlers on the mole to take up her anchor and to be hoisting sail. Before the freshening breeze that set a sparkling ruffle on the sunlit violet waters, she moved majestically eastward along the peninsula on which San Juan is built.

Penmanship had occupied some of Captain Blood's time aboard since yesterday, and the Admiral's writing-coffer had supplied his needs: the Admiral's seal and a sheet of parchment surmounted by the arms of Spain.

Hence an imposing document, which he now placed before Don Sebastian. Explanations plausibly accompanied it.

'Your assurance that Captain Blood is in these waters has persuaded the Admiral to hunt him out. In his excellency's absence, he commands me, as you observe, to remain here.'

The Captain-General was poring over the parchment with its great slab of red wax bearing the arms of the Marquis of Riconete. It ordered Don Sebastian to make over to Don Pedro Encarnado the command of the military establishment of San Juan de Puerto Rico, the fort of Santo Antonio and its garrison.

It was not an order that Don Sebastian could be expected to receive with equanimity. He frowned and blew out his fat lips.

'I do not understand this at all. Colonel Vargas, who commands the fort under my orders, is a competent, experienced officer. Besides,' he bristled, 'I have been under the impression that it is I who am Captain-General of Puerto Rico, and that it is for me to appoint my officers.'

No speech or manner could have been more conciliatory than Captain Blood's.

'In your place, Don Sebastian, I must confess—oh, but entirely between ourselves—that I should feel precisely as you do. But . . . What would you? It is necessary to have patience. The Admiral is moved to excessive anxiety for the safety of the plate ships.'

'Is not their safety in San Juan my affair? Am I not the King's representative in Puerto Rico? Let the Admiral command as he pleases on the ocean; but here on land . . .'

Suavely Captain Blood interrupted him, a hand familiarly upon his shoulder.

'My dear Don Sebastian!' He lowered his voice to a confidential tone. 'You know how it is with these royal favourites.'

'Royal . . .' Don Sebastian choked down his annoyance in sudden apprehension. 'I never heard that the Marquis of Riconete is a royal favourite.'

'A lapdog to His Majesty. That, of course, between ourselves. Hence his audacity. I should not blame you for holding the opinion that he abuses the King's affection for him. You know how the royal favour goes to a man's head.' He paused and sighed. 'It distresses me to be the instrument of this encroachment upon your province. But I am as helpless as yourself, my friend.'

Thus brought to imagine that he trod dangerous ground, Don Sebastian suppressed the heat begotten of this indignity to his office, and philosophically consented, as Captain Blood urged him, to take comfort in the thought that the Admiral's interference possessed at least the advantage for him of relieving him of all responsibility for what might follow.

After this, and in the two succeeding days, Peter Blood displayed a tact that made things easy, not only for the Captain-General, but also for Colonel Vargas, who at first had been disposed to verbal violence on the subject of his supersession. It reconciled the Colonel, at least in part, to discover that the new commandant showed no inclination to interfere with any of his military measures. Far from it, having made a close inspection of the fort, its armament, garrison, and munitions, he warmly commended all that he beheld, and generously confessed that he should not know how to improve upon the Colonel's dispositions.

It was on the first Friday in June that the false Don Pedro had come ashore to take command. On the following Sunday morning in the courtyard of the Captain-General's quarters, a breathless young officer reeled from the saddle of a lathered, spent, and quivering horse. To Don Sebastian, who was at breakfast with his lady and his temporary commandant, this messenger brought the alarming news that a powerfully armed ship that flew no flag and was manifestly a pirate was threatening San Patrico, fifty miles away. It had opened a bombardment of the settlement, so far without damage because it dared not come within range of the fire maintained by the guns of the harbour fort. Lamentably, however, the fort was very short of ammunition, and once this were exhausted there was no adequate force in men to resist a landing.

Such was Don Sebastian's amazement that it transcended his alarm.

'In the Devil's name, what should pirates seek at San Patrico? There's nothing there but sugar-cane and maize.'

'I think I understand,' said Captain Blood. 'San Patrico is the back door to San Juan and the plate ships.'

'The back door?'

'Don't you see? Because these pirates dare not venture a frontal attack against your heavily armed fort of Santo Antonio here, they hope to march overland from San Patrico and take you in the rear.'

The Captain-General was profoundly impressed by this prompt display of military acumen.

'By all the Saints, I believe you explain it.' He heaved himself up, announcing that he would take order at once, dismissed the officer to rest and refreshment, and despatched a messenger to fetch Colonel Vargas from the fort.

Stamping up and down the long room, which was kept in cool shadow by the slatted blinds, he gave thanks to his patron saint, the martyred centurion, that Santo Antonio was abundantly munitioned, thanks to his foresight, and could spare all the powder and shot that San Patrico might require so as to hold these infernal pirates at bay.

The timid glance of Doña Leocadia followed him about the room, then was turned upon the new commandant when his voice cool and calm, invaded the Captain-General's pause for breath.

'With submission, sir, it would be an error to take munitions from Santo Antonio. We may require all that we have. Several things are possible. These buccaneers may change their plans when they find the landing at San Patrico less easy than they suppose. Or'—and now he stated what he knew to be the case, since it was precisely what he had commanded—'Or the attack on San Patrico may be no more than a feint, to draw thither your strength.'

Don Sebastian stared blankly, passing a jewelled hand over his ponderous blue jowl. 'That is possible. Yes, God help me!' And thankful now for the presence of this calm, discerning commandant, whose coming at first had so offended him, he cast himself entirely upon the man's resourcefulness.

Don Pedro was prompt to take command. 'I have a note of the munitions aboard the plate ships. They are considerable. Abundant for the needs of San Patrico, and useless at present to the vessels. We will take not only their powder and shot, but their guns as well, and haul them at once to San Patrico.'

'You'll disarm the plate ships?' Don Sebastian stared alarm.

'What need to keep them armed whilst in harbour here? It is the fort that will defend the entrance if it should come to need defending. The emergency is at San Patrico.' He became more definite. 'You will be good enough to order the necessary mules and oxen for the transport. As for men there are two hundred and thirty at Santo Antonio and a hundred and twenty aboard the plate ships. What is the force at San Patrico?'

'Between forty and fifty.'

'God help us! If these buccaneers intend a landing, it follows that they must be four or five hundred strong. To oppose them San Patrico will need every man we can spare. I shall have to send Colonel Vargas thither with a hundred and fifty men from Santo Antonio and a hundred men from the ships.'

'And leave San Juan defenceless?' In his horror Don Sebastian could not help adding: 'Are you mad?'

Captain Blood's air was that of a man whose knowledge of his business places him beyond all wavering. 'I think not. We have the fort with a hundred guns, half of them of powerful calibre. A hundred men should abundantly suffice to serve them. And lest you suppose that I subject you to risks I am not prepared to share, I shall, myself, remain here to command them.'

When Vargas came, he was as horrified as Don Sebastian at this depletion of the defence of San Juan. In the heat of his arguments against it he became almost discourteous. He looked down his nose at the Admiral's deputy, and spoke of the Art of War as if from an eminence where it had no secrets. From that eminence, the new commandant coolly dislodged him.

'If you tell me that we can attempt to resist a landing at San Patrico with fewer than three hundred men, I shall understand that you have still to learn the elements of your profession. And, anyway,' he added, rising, so as to mark the end of the discussion, 'I have the honour to command here, and the responsibility is mine. I shall be glad if you will give my orders your promptest obedience.'

Colonel Vargas bowed stiffly, biting his lip, and the Captain-General returned explosive thanks to Heaven that he held a parchment from the Admiral of the Ocean-Sea which must relieve him of all blame for whatever consequences might attend this rashness.

As the cathedral bells were summoning the faithful to High Mass, and notwithstanding the approaching sweltering heat of noontide, the matter admitting of no delay, Colonel Vargas marched his men out of San Juan. At the head of the column, and followed by a long train of mules, laden with ammunition, and of oxen-teams hauling the guns, the Colonel took the road across the gently undulating plains to San Patrico, fifty miles away.

3

You will have conceived that the pirate threatening San Patrico was the erstwhile flaship of the Spanish Admiral of the Ocean-Sea, now the *Andalusian Lass,* despatched thither on that business by Captain Blood. Wolverstone had been placed in command of her, and his orders were to maintain his demonstration and keep the miserable little fort of San Patrico in play for forty-eight hours. At the end of that time, and under cover of night, he was to slip quietly away before the arrival of the reinforcements from San Juan, which by then would be well upon their way, and abandoning the feint, come round at speed to deliver the real blow at the now comparatively defenceless San Juan.

Messengers from San Patrico arriving at regular intervals throughout Monday brought reports that showed how faithfully Wolverstone was fulfilling his instructions. The messages gave assurance that the constant fire of the fort was compelling the pirates to keep their distance.

It was heartening news to the Captain-General, persuaded that every hour that passed increased the chances that the raiders would be caught red-handed by the Admiral of the Ocean-Sea, who must be somewhere in the neighbourhood, and incontinently destroyed.

'By tomorrow,' he said, 'Vargas will be at San Patrico with the reinforcements and the pirates' chance of landing will be at an end.'

But what the morrow brought was something very different from the expectations of all concerned. Soon after daybreak, San Juan was awakened by the roar of guns. Don Sebastian's first uplifting thought, as he thrust a leg out of bed, was that here was the Marquis of Riconete announcing his return by a fully royal salute. The continuous bombardment, however, stirred his misgivings even before he reached the terrace of his fine house. Once there, and having seen what his telescope could show him in detail, his misgivings were changed to stark consternation.

Captain Blood's first awakening emotions had been the very opposite to Don Sebastian's. But his annoyed assumptions were at once dismissed. Even if Wolverstone should have left San Patrico before midnight, which was unlikely, it was impossible, in the teeth of the keen westerly wind now blowing, that he could reach San Juan for another twelve hours. Moreover, Wolverstone was not the man to act in such careless disregard of his instructions.

Half-dressed, Captain Blood made haste to seek at Don Sebastian's side the explanation of this artillery, and there experienced a consternation no whit inferior to the Captain-General's, though vastly different of source. For the great red ship whose guns were pounding the fort from the roads, a half-mile away, had all the appearance of his own *Arabella,* which he had left careened in Tortuga less than a month ago.

He remembered the false current tale of a raid by Captain Blood on Cartagena, and he asked himself was it possible that Pitt and Dyke and other associates whom he had left behind had gone roving in his absence, conducting their raids with inhuman cruelties such as those which had disgraced Morgan and Montbars. He could not believe it of them; and yet here stood his ship under a billowing cloud of smoke from her own gunfire, delivering broadsides that were bringing down the walls of a fort that had the appearance of being massive and substantial, but the mortar of which, as he had been glad to ascertain when inspecting it, was mere adobe.

At his side the Captain-General of Puerto Rico was invoking alternately all the saints in the calendar and all the fiends in Hell to bear witness that here was that incarnate devil Captain Blood.

Tight-lipped, that incarnate devil at his very elbow gave no heed to his imprecations. With a hand to his brow, so as to shade his eyes from the morning sun, he scanned the lines of that red ship from gilded beak-head to towering poop. It was the *Arabella,* and yet it was not the *Arabella.* The difference eluded him, yet a difference he perceived.

As he looked, the great vessel came broadside on in the act of going about. Then, even without counting her gun-ports, he obtained a clear assurance. She carried four guns less than his own flagship.

'That is not Captain Blood,' he said.

'Not Captain Blood? You'll tell me that I am not Sebastian Mendes. Is not his ship named the *Arabella?'*

'That is not the *Arabella.*'

Don Sebastian looked him over with a contemptuous, blood-injected eye. Then he proffered his telescope.

'Read the name on the counter for yourself.'

Captain Blood took the glass. The ship was swinging, so as to bring her starboard guns to bear, and her counter came fully into view. In letters of gold, he read there the name *Arabella,* and his bewilderment was renewed.

'I do not understand,' he said. But the roar of her broadside drowned his words and loosened some further tons of the fort's masonry. And then, at last, the guns of the fort thundered in their turn for the first time. The fire was wild and wide of the mark, but at least it had the effect of compelling the attacking ship to stand off, so as to get out of range.

'By God, they're awake at last!' cried Don Sebastian, with bitter irony.

Blood departed in search of his boots, ordering the scared servants who stood about to find and saddle him a horse.

When five minutes later, booted, but still not more than half-dressed, he was setting his foot to the stirrup, the Captain-General surged beside him.

'It's your responsibility,' he raged. 'Yours and your precious Admiral's. Your fatuous measures have left us defenceless. I hope you'll be able to answer for it. I hope so.'

'I hope so, too; and to that brigand, whoever he may be.'

Captain Blood spoke through his teeth in an anger more bitter if less boisterous than the Captain-General's. For he was experiencing the condition of being hoist with his own petard and all the emotions that accompany it. He had been at such elaborate and crafty pains to disarm San Juan, merely, it seemed, so as to make it easy for a pestilential interloper to come and snatch from under his very nose the prize for which he played. He could not conjecture the identity of the interloper, but he had more than a suspicion that it was not by mere coincidence that this red ship was named the

Arabella, and not a doubt but that her master was the author of those horrors in Cartagena which were being assigned to Captain Blood.

However that might be, what mattered now was do what might be done so as to frustrate this most inopportune of interlopers. And so, by a singular irony, Captain Blood rode forth upon the hope, rendered forlorn by his own contriving, of organizing the defences of a Spanish place against an attack by buccaneers.

He found the fortress in a state of desolation and confusion. Half the guns were already out of action under the heaped rubble. Of the hundred men that had been left to garrison it, ten had been killed and thirty disabled. The sixty that remained whole were resolute and steady men—there were no better troops in the world than those of the Spanish infantry—but reduced to helplessness by the bewildered incompetence of the young officer in command.

Captain Blood came amongst them just as another broadside shore away twenty yards of ramparts. In the well-like courtyard, half-choked with the dust of crumbling masonry and the acrid fumes of gunpowder, he stormed at the officer who ran to meet him.

'Will you keep your company cowering here until men and guns are all buried together in these ruins?'

Captain Araña bridled. He threw a chest. 'We can die at our posts, sir, to pay for your errors.'

'So can any fool. But if you had as much intelligence as impertinence you would be saving some of the guns. They'll be needed presently. Haul a score of them out of this, and have them posted in that cover.' He pointed to a pimento grove less than a half-mile away in the direction of the city. 'Leave me a dozen hands to serve the guns that remain, and take every other man with you. And get your wounded out of this death-trap. When you're in the grove, send out for teams of mules, horses, oxen, what you will, against the need for further haulage. Load with canister. Use your wits, man, and waste no time. About it.'

If Captain Araña lacked imagination to conceive, at

least he possessed energy to execute the conceptions of another. Dominated by the commandant's brisk authority, fired by admiration for measures whose simple soundness he at once perceived, he went diligently to work, whilst Blood took charge of a battery of ten guns emplaced on the southern rampart which best commanded the bay. A dozen men, aroused from their inertia by his vigour, and stimulated by his own indifference to danger, carried out his orders calmly and swiftly.

The buccaneer, having emptied her starboard guns, was going about so as to bring her larboard broadside to bear. Taking advantage of the manoeuvre, and gauging as best he could the station from which her next fire would be delivered, Blood passed from gun to gun, laying each with his own hands, deliberately and carefully. He had just laid the last of them when the red ship, having put the helm over, presented her larboard flank. He snatched the spluttering match from the hand of a musketeer, and instantly touched off the gun at that broad target. If the shot was not as lucky as he hoped, yet it was lucky enough. It shore away the pirate's bowsprit. She yawed under the shock and listed slightly, and this at the very moment that her broadside was delivered. As a consequence of that fortuitously altered elevation, the discharge soared harmlessly over the fort and went to plough the ground in its rear. At once she swung down wind so as to run out of range.

'Fire!' roared Blood, and the other nine guns blazed as one.

The buccaneer's stern presenting but a narrow mark, Blood could hope for little more than a moral effect. But again luck favoured him, and if eight of the twenty-four-pound missiles merely flung up the spray about the ship, the ninth crashed into her stern-coach, to speed her on her way.

The Spaniards sent up a cheer. 'Viva Don Pedro!' And it was actually with laughter that they set about reloading, their courage resurrected by that first if slight success.

There was no need now for haste. It took the buccaneer some time to clear the wreckage of her bowsprit,
and it was quite an hour before she was beating back,
close-hauled against the breeze, to take her revenge.

In that most valuable respite, Araña had got the guns
into the cover of the grove a quarter of a mile away.
Thither Blood might have retreated to join him. But,
greatly daring, he stayed, first to repeat his earlier tactics. This time, however, his fire went wide, and the
full force of the red ship's broadside came smashing
into the fort to open another wound in its crumbling
flank. Then, infuriated perhaps by the mishap suffered,
and judging, no doubt, from the fort's previous volley
that only a few of its guns remained effective and that
these would now be empty, the buccaneer ran in close,
and, going about, delivered her second broadside at
point-blank range.

The result was an explosion that shook the buildings
in San Juan, a mile away.

Blood felt as if giant hands had seized him, lifted
him, and cast him violently from them upon the subsiding ground. He lay winded and half-stunned, while
rubble came spattering down in a Titanic hailstorm,
and to the roar as of a continuous cataract, the walls of
the fort slid down as if suddenly turned liquid, and came
to rest in a shapeless heap of ruin.

An unlucky shot had found the powder magazine. It
was the end of the fort.

The cheer that came over the water from the buccaneer ship was like an echo of the explosion.

Blood roused himself, shook himself free of the
mortar and rubble in which he was half-buried, coughed
the dust from his throat, and made a mental examina-
tion of his condition. His hip was hurt, but the gradually subsiding pain assured him that there was no
permanent damage. He got slowly to his knees, still
half-dazed, then at last to his feet. Badly shaken, his
hands cut and bleeding, smothered in dust and grime,
he was, at least, whole. He had broken nothing. But of
the twelve who had been with him he found only five as

sound as they had been before the explosion; a sixth lay groaning with a broken thigh, a seventh sat nursing a dislocated shoulder. The other five were gone, buried in that heaped-up mound.

He collected wits that had been badly scattered, straightened his dusty periwig, and decided that there could be no purpose in lingering on this rubbish heap that lately had been a fort. To the five survivors he ordered the care of their two crippled fellows, saw these borne away towards the pimento grove, and went staggering after them.

By the time he reached the shelter of that belt of perfumed trees, the buccaneers were disposing for the tactics that logically followed upon the destruction of the fort. Their preparations for landing were clearly discernible to Blood as he paused on the edge of the grove to observe them, shading his eyes from the glare of the sun. He saw that five boats had been lowered, and that, manned to overcrowding, these were pulling away for the beach, whilst the red ship rode now at anchor to cover the landing.

There was no time to lose. Blood entered the cool, green shade of the plantation, where Araña and his men awaited him. He approved the emplacement there of the guns unsuspected by the buccaneers, and charged with canister as he had directed. Carefully judging the spot, less than a mile away, where the enemy should come ashore, he ordered and himself supervised the training of the guns upon it. He took for mark a fishing boat that stood upside down upon the beach, half a cable's length from the water's creamy edge.

'We'll wait,' he explained to Araña, 'until those sons of dogs are in line with it, and then we'll give them a passport into Hell.'

From that, so as to beguile the waiting moments, he went on to lecture the Spanish captain upon the finer details of the art of war.

'You begin to perceive the advantages that may lie in departing from school-room rules and preconceptions, and in abandoning a fort that can't be held, so as

to improvise another one that can be. By these tactics
we hold those ruffians at our mercy. In a moment you'll
see them swept to perdition, and victory plucked from
the appearance of defeat.'

No doubt it is what would have happened but for the
supervention of the unexpected. As a matter of fact,
Captain Araña was having an even more instructive
morning than Captain Blood intended. He was now to
receive a demonstration of the futility of divided command.

4

The trouble came from Don Sebastian who, meanwhile, had unfortunately not been idle. As Captain-General of Puerto Rico he conceived it to be his duty to
arm every man of the town who was able to lift a
weapon. Without taking the precaution of consulting
Don Pedro, or even of informing him of what he proposed, he had brought the improvised army, some five
or six score strong, under cover of the white buildings,
to within a hundred yards of the water. There he held
them in ambush, to launch them in a charge against the
landing buccaneers, at the very last moment. In this way
he calculated to make it impossible for the ship's artillery to play upon his force, and he was exultantly
proud of his tactical conception.

In themselves these tactics were as sound as they
were obvious; but they suffered from the unsuspected
disadvantage that whilst they baulked the buccaneer
gunners on the ship, they no less baulked the Spanish
battery in the grove. Before Blood could deliver the fire
he was holding, he beheld to his dismay the yelling improvised army of Puerto-Rican townsfolk go charging
down the beach upon the invader, so that in a moment
all was a heaving, writhing, battling, screaming press, in
which friend and foe were inextricably mixed.

In this confusion that fighting mob surged up the
beach, slowly at first, but steadily gathering impetus, in

a measure as Don Sebastian's forces gave way before the fury of little more than half their number of buccaneers. Firing and shouting they all vanished together into the town, leaving some bodies behind them on the sands.

Whilst Captain Blood was cursing Don Sebastian's untimely interference, Captain Araña was urging a rescue. He received yet another lesson.

'Battles are not won by heroics, my friend, but by calculation. The ruffians aboard will number at least twice those that have been landed; and these are by now masters of the situation, thanks to the heroics of Don Sebastian. If we march in now, we shall be taken in the rear by the next landing party, and thus find ourselves caught between two fires. So we'll wait, if you please, for the second landing party, and when we've destroyed that, we'll deal with the blackguards who are by now in possession of the town. Thus we make sure.'

The time of waiting, however, was considerable. In each of the boats only two men had been left to pull back to the ship, and their progress was slow. Slow, too, was the second loading and return. So that close upon two hours had passed since the first landing before the second party leapt ashore.

It may have appeared to this second party that there was no need for haste, since all the signs went clearly to show that the feeble opposition offered by San Juan had already been fully overcome.

Therefore, no haste they made even when their heels grated on the beach. In leisurely fashion they climbed out of the boats, a motley crowd, like that which had composed the first landing-party: some in hats, some few in morions, others with heads swathed in dirty, gaudy scarves, and offering the same variety in the remainder of their dress. It was representative of every class, from the frank buccaneer in cotton shirt and rawhide breeches to the hidalgo in a laced coat, whilst here and there a back-and-breast supplied a more military equipment. They were uniform at least in that everybody was scarved by a bandoleer, every shoulder bore a musket, and from every belt hung a sword of some description.

They numbered perhaps fifty, and one who seemed set in authority and wore a gaudy scarlet coat with tarnished lace, marshalled them at the water's edge into a parody of military formation, then, placing himself at their head, waved his sword and gave the word to march.

They marched, breaking into song, so as to supply a rhythm. Raucously bawling their lewd ditty they advanced in close order, whilst in the pimento grove the gunners blew on their matches, their eyes on Captain Blood who watched and waited, his right arm raised. At last the raiders were in line with the boat which had served the Spaniards for a mark. Blood's arm fell, and five guns were touched off as one.

That hail of canister swept away the head of the column together with the sword-waving leader in his fine red coat. The unexpectedness of the blow struck the remainder with a sudden palsy, from which few recovered in time. For twice more did Blood's arm rise and fall, and twice more did the charge of five guns mow through those too serried ranks, until almost all that remained of them were heaped about the beach below, some writhing and some still. A few, a half-dozen, perhaps, escaped miraculously whole and unscathed, and these, not daring to return to the boats which stood unmanned and empty where they had been drawn up, were making for the shelter of the town, and wriggling on their stomachs lest another murderous blast should sweep death across that beach. Captain Blood smiled terribly into the startled eyes of Captain Araña. He resumed the military education of that worthy Spanish officer.

'We may advance now with confidence, Captain, since we have made our rear secure from attack. You may have observed that with deplorable rashness the pirates have employed all their boats in their landings. What men remain aboard that ship are safety marooned in her.'

'But they have guns,' objected Araña. 'What if in vindictiveness they open fire upon the town?'

'Whilst their captain and his first landing party are in it? Not likely. Still, so as to make sure, we'll leave a dozen men here to serve these guns. If those on board should turn desperate and lose their heads, a volley or two will drive them out of range.'

Dispositions made, an orderly company of fifty Spanish musketeers, unsuspected by the buccaneers to have survived the demolition of the fort, were advancing from the pimento grove at the double upon the town.

5

The pirate captain—whose name has not survived—was set down by Blood as a lubberly idiot, who like all idiots took too much for granted, otherwise he would have taken the precaution to make sure that the force which had opposed his landing comprised the full strength of San Juan. Ludicrous, too, was the grasping covetousness which had inspired that landing. In this Captain Blood accounted him just a cheap thief, who stayed to rake up crumbs where a feast was spread. With the great prize for which the scoundrel played, the two treasure-ships which he had chased across the Caribbean from Cartagena, now lying all but at his mercy, it was a stupid rashness not to have devoted all his energy to making himself master of them at once. From the circumstance that those ships had never fired a gun, he must have inferred—if he was capable of inferences—that the crews were ashore; and if he was not capable of inferences, his telescope—and Captain Blood supposed that the fellow would at least possess a telescope—should have enabled him to ascertain the fact by observation.

But here Blood's reasoning is at fault. For it may well have been the actual perception that the ships were unmanned and easily to be reduced into possession which induced the captain to let them wait until his excessive greed should have been satisfied by the plunder of the town. After all, he will have remembered, there was often great store of wealth in these cities of New Spain, and there would be a royal treasury in the keeping of the Governor. It would be just such a temptation as this which had led him to plunder the city of Cartagena whilst those treasure-ships were putting to sea. Evidently not even this had sufficed to teach him that who seeks to grasp too much ends by holding nothing; and here he was in San Juan pursuing the same inexpert methods, and pursuing them in the same disgusting manner as that in which at Cartagena he had dishonoured—as Captain Blood was now fully persuaded—the name of the great buccaneer leader which he had assumed.

I will not say that in what he had done Captain Blood was not actuated by the determination that no interloper should come and snatch from him the prize for which he had laboured and the capture of which his dispositions had rendered easy, but I account it beyond doubt that his manner of doing it gathered an unusual ferocity because of his deep resentment of that foul impersonation at Cartagena and the horrors perpetrated there in his name. The sins of a career which harsh fortune had imposed upon him were heavy enough already. He could not patiently suffer that still worse offences should be attributed to him as a result of the unrestrained methods of this low pretender and his crew of ruthless blackguards.

So it was a grimly resolute, not to say a vindictive Captain Blood who marched that little column of Spanish musketeers to clean up a place which his impersonator would now be defiling. As they approached the town gate, the sounds that met them abundantly justified his assumptions of the nature of the raider's activities.

The buccaneer captain had swept invincibly through a place whose resistance had been crushed at the outset. Finding it at his mercy, he had delivered it to his men for pillage. Let them make holiday here awhile in their brutal fashion before settling down to the main business of the raid and possessing themselves of the plate ships in the harbour. And so that evil crew, composed of the scourings of the gaols of every land, had broken up into groups which had scattered through the town on a voluptuous course of outrage: smashing, burning, pillaging, and murdering in sheer lust of destruction.

For himself the leader marked down what should prove the richest prize in San Juan. With a half-dozen followers he broke into the house of the Captain-General, where Don Sebastian had shut himself up after the rout of his inopportunely improvised force.

Having laid violent hands upon Don Sebastian and his comely, panic-stricken little lady, the captain delivered over the main plunder of the house to the men who were with him. Two of these, however, he retained, to assist him in the particular kind of robbery upon which he was intent, whilst the other four were left remorselessly to pillage the Spaniard's property and guzzle the fine wines that he had brought from Spain.

A tall, swarthy, raffish fellow of not more than thirty, who had announced himself as Captain Blood, and who flaunted the black and silver that was notoriously Blood's common wear, the pirate sprawled at his ease in Don Sebastian's dining-room. He sat at the head of the long table of dark oak, one leg hooked over the arm of his chair, his plumed hat cocked over one eye, and a leer on his thick, shaven lips.

Opposite to him, at the table's foot, between two of the captain's ruffians, stood Don Sebastian in shirt and breeches, without his wig, his hands pinioned behind him, his face the colour of lead, yet with defiance in his dark eyes.

Midway between them, but away from the table, in a tall chair, with her back to one of the open windows, sat Doña Leocadia in a state of terror that brought her to the verge of physical sickness, but otherwise robbed her of movement.

The captain's fingers were busy with a length of whipcord, making knots in it. In slow, mocking tones and in clumsy, scarcely intelligible Spanish, he addressed his victim.

'So you won't talk, eh? You'ld put me to the trouble of pulling down this damned hovel of yours stone by stone, so as to find what I want. Your error, my hidalgo. You'll not only talk, you'll be singing presently. Here's to provide the music.'

He flung the knotted whipcord up the table, signing to one of his men to take and use it. In a moment it was tightly encircling the Captain-General's brow, and the grinning ape whose dirty fingers had bound it there took up a silver spoon from the Spaniard's sideboard, and passed the handle of it between the cord and the flesh.

'Hold there,' his captain bade him. 'Now, Don Gubernador, you know what's coming if you don't loose your obstinate tongue and tell me where you hide your pieces of eight.' He paused, watching the Spaniard from under lowered eyelids, a curl of contemptuous amusement on his lip. 'If you prefer it, we can give you a lighted match between the fingers, or a hot iron to the soles of your feet. We've all manner of ingenious miracles for restoring speech to the dumb. It's as you please, my friend. But you'll gain nothing by being mute. Come, now. These doubloons. Where do you hide them?'

But the Spaniard, his head high, his lips tight, glared at him in silent detestation.

The pirate's smile broadened in deepening contemptuous menace. He sighed.

'Well, well! I'm a patient man. You shall have a minute to think it over. One minute.' He held up a dirty forefinger. 'Time for me to drink this.' He poured himself a bumper of dark syrupy Malaga from a silver jug, and quaffed it at a draught. He set down the lovely glass so violently that the stem snapped. He used it as an illustration. 'And that's how I'll serve your ugly neck in the end, you Spanish pimp, if you play the mule with me. Now, then: these doubloons. *Vamos, maldito! Soy Don Pedro Sangre, yo!* Haven't you heard that you can't trifle with Captain Blood?'

Hate continued to glare at him from Don Sebastian's eyes.

'I've heard nothing of you that's as obscene as the reality, you foul pirate dog. I tell you nothing.'

The lady stirred, and made a whimpering, incoherent sound, that presently resolved itself into speech.

'For pity's sake, Sebastian! In God's name, tell him. Tell him. Let him take all we have. What does it matter?'

'What, indeed, if you've no life with which to enjoy it?' the captain mocked him. 'Give heed to your pullet's better sense. No?' He banged the table in anger. 'So be it! Squeeze it out of his cuckoldy head, my lads.' And he settled himself more comfortably in his chair, in expectation of entertainment.

One of the brigands laid hands upon the spoon he had thrust between cord and brow. But before he had begun to twist it, the captain checked him again.

'Wait. There's perhaps a surer way.' He laughed, unhooked his leg from the chair-arm, and sat up. 'These dons be mighty proud o' their women.' He turned, and beckoned Doña Leocadia. '*Aqui, muger! Aqui!*' he commanded.

'Don't heed him, Leocadia,' cried her husband. 'Don't move.'

'He . . . he can always fetch me,' she answered, pathetically practical in her disobedience.

'You hear, fool? It's a pity you've none of her good sense. Come along, madam.'

The frail, pallid little woman, quaking with fear, dragged herself to the side of his chair. He looked up at her with his odious smile, and in his close-set eyes there was insulting appraisal of this dainty, timid wisp of womanhood. He flung an arm about her waist, and pulled her to him.

'Come closer, woman. What the devil!'

Don Sebastian closed his eyes, and groaned between pain and fury. For a moment he strove desperately in the powerful hands that held him.

The captain, handling the little lady as if she were invertebrate, as indeed horror had all but rendered her, hauled her to sit upon his knee.

'Never heed his jealous bellowing, little one. He shan't harm you, on the word of Captain Blood.' He tilted up her chin, and smiled into dark eyes that panic was dilating. This and his lingering kiss she bore as a corpse might have borne them. 'There'll be more o' that to follow, my pullet, unless your loutish husband comes to his senses. I've got her, you see, Don Gubernador, and I dare swear she'ld enjoy a voyage with me. But you can ransom her with the doubloons you hide. You'll allow that's generous, now. For I can help myself to both if I've a mind to it.'

The threatened woolding could not have put Don Sebastian in a greater anguish.

'You dog! Even if I yield, what assurance have I that you will keep faith?'

'The word of Captain Blood.'

A sudden burst of gunfire shook the house. It was closely followed by a second and yet a third.

Momentarily it startled them.

'What the devil . . .' the captain was beginning, when he checked, prompt to find the explanation. 'Bah! My children amuse themselves. That's all.'

But he would hardly have laughed as heartily as he did, could he have guessed that those bursts of gunfire had mown down some fifty of those children of his, in the very act of landing to reinforce him, or that some fifty Spanish musketeers were advancing at the double from the pimento grove, led by the authentic Captain Blood, who came to deal with the pirates scattered through the town. And deal with them he did with sharp efficiency, in a measure as he came upon them in groups of four, or six, or ten at most. Some were shot at sight, and the remainder rounded up and taken prisoners, so that no chance was ever theirs to assemble and offer an organized resistance.

In the Captain-General's dining-room, the buccaneer captain, unhurried because deriving more and more evil relish from the situation in a measure as he grew more fuddled by the heady Malaga wine, gave little heed to the increasing sounds outside, the shots, the screams, and the bursts of musketry. In his complete persuasion that all power of resistance had been crushed, he supposed these to be the ordinary indications that his children continued to amuse themselves. Idle gunfire was a common practice among jubilant filibusters, and who but his own men should now have muskets to fire in San Juan?

So he continued at his leisure to savour the voluptuous humour of tormenting the Captain-General with a choice between losing his wife or his doubloons until at last Don Sebastian's spirit broke, and he told them where the King's treasure-chest was stored.

But the evil in the buccaneer was not allayed. 'Too late,' he declared. 'You've been trifling with me overlong. And in the meantime I've grown fond of this dainty piece of yours. So fond that I couldn't bear now to be parted from her. Your life you may have, you Spanish dog. And after your cursed obstinacy that's more than you deserve. But your money and your woman go with me, like the plate ships of the King of Spain.'

'You pledged me your word!' cried the demented Spaniard.

'Ah, ay! But that was long since. You didn't accept when the chance was yours. You chose to trifle with me.' Thus the filibuster mocked him, and in the room none heeded the quick approach of steps. 'And I warned you that it is not safe to trifle with Captain Blood.'

The last word was not out of him when the door was flung open, and a crisp, metallic voice was answering him on a grimly humorous note.

'Faith, I'm glad to hear you say it, whoever you may be.'

A tall man in a dishevelled black periwig, without a hat, his violet coat in rags, his lean face smeared with sweat and grime, came in sword in hand. At his heels followed three musketeers in Spanish corselets and steel caps. The sweep of his glance took in the situation.

'So. So. No more than in time, I think.'

Startled, the ruffian flung Doña Leocadia from him

and bounded to his feet, a hand on one of the pistols
he carried slung before him at the ends of an em-
broidered stole.

'What's this? In Hell's name, who are you?'

The newcomer stepped close to him and out of that
begrimed countenance eyes blue as sapphires and as
hard sent a chill through him.

'You poor pretender! You dung-souled impostor!'

Whatever the ruffian may or may not have understood, he was in no doubt that here was need for instant action. He plucked forth the pistol on which his
hand was resting. But before he could level it, Captain
Blood had stepped back. His rapier licked forth, sudden
as a viper's tongue, to transfix the pirate's arm, and the
pistol clattered from a nerveless hand.

'You should have had it in the heart, you dog, but
for a vow I've made that, God helping me, Captain
Blood shall never be hanged by any hand but mine.'

One of the musketeers closed with the disabled man,
and bore him down, snarling and cursing, whilst Blood
and the others dealt swiftly and efficiently with his men.

Above the din of that brief struggle rang the scream
of Doña Leocadia, who reeled to a chair, fell into it,
and fainted.

Don Sebastian, scarcely in better case when his bonds
were cut, babbled weakly, an incoherent mixture of
thanksgivings for this timely miracle and questions upon
how it had been wrought.

'Look to your lady,' Blood advised him, 'and give
yourself no other thought. San Juan is cleared of this
blight. Some thirty of these scoundrels are safe in the
town gaol, the others, safer still, in Hell. If any have got
away at all, they'll find a party waiting for them at the
boats. We've the dead to bury, the wounded to attend,
the fugitives from the town to recall. Look to your lady
and your household, and leave the rest to me.'

He was away again, as abruptly as he had come, and
gone too were his musketeers bearing the raging captive
with them.

6

He came back at supper-time to find order restored to the Captain-General's house, the servants at their posts once more, and the table spread. Doña Leocadia burst into tears at sight of him, still all begrimed from battle. Don Sebastian hugged him to his ample bosom, the grime notwithstanding, proclaiming him the saviour of San Juan, a hero of the true Castilian pattern, a worthy representative of the great Admiral of the Ocean-Sea. And this, too, was the opinion of the town, which resounded that night with cries of 'Viva Don Pedro! Long live the hero of San Juan de Puerto Rico!'

It was all very pleasant and touching, and induced in Captain Blood, as he afterwards confessed to Jeremy Pitt, a mood of reflection upon the virtue of service to the cause of law and order. Cleansed and reclothed, in garments at once too loose and too short, borrowed from Don Sebastian's wardrobe, he sat down to supper at the Captain-General's table, ate heartily and did justice to some excellent Spanish wine that had survived the raid upon the Captain-General's cellar.

He slept peacefully, in the consciousness of a good action performed and the assurance that, being without boats and very short of men, the pretended *Arabella* was powerless to accomplish upon the treasure-ships the real object of her descent upon San Juan. So as to make doubly sure, however, a Spanish company kept watch at the guns in the pimento grove. But there was no alarm, and when day broke it showed them the pirate ship hull down on the horizon, and in a majesty of full sail, the sometime '*Maria Gloriosa*' entering the roads.

At breakfast, when he came to it, Don Pedro Encarnado was greeted by Don Sebastian with news that his Admiral's ship had just dropped anchor in the bay.

'He is very punctual,' said Don Pedro, thinking of Wolverstone.

'Punctual? He's behind the fair. He arrives just too

late to complete your glorious work by sinking that pirate craft. I shall hope to tell him so.'

Don Pedro frowned. 'That would be imprudent, considering his favour with the King. It is not well to ruffle the Marquis. Fortunately he is not likely to come ashore. The gout, you see.'

'But I shall pay him a visit aboard his ship.'

There was no make-believe in Captain Blood's frown. Unless he could turn Don Sebastian from that reasonable intention the smooth plan he had evolved would be disastrously wrecked.

'No, no. I shouldn't do that,' he said.

'Not do it? Of course I shall. It is my duty.'

'Oh, no, no. You would derogate. Think of the great position you occupy. Captain-General of Puerto Rico; which is to say, Governor, Viceroy almost. It is not for you to wait upon admirals, but for admirals to wait upon you. And the Marquis of Riconete is well aware of it. That is why, being unable, from his plaguey gout, to come in person, he sent me to be his deputy. What you have to say to the Marquis, you can say here, at your ease, to me.'

Impressed, Don Sebastian passed a reflective hand over his several chins.

'There is, of course, a certain truth in what you say. Yes, yes. Nevertheless, in this case I have a special duty to perform, which must be performed in person. I must acquaint the Admiral very fully with the heroic part you have played in saving Puerto Rico and the King's treasury here, not to mention the plate ships. Honour where honour is due. I must see, Don Pedro, that you have your deserts.'

And Doña Leocadia, remembering with a shudder the horrors of yesterday which the gallantry of Don Pedro had cut short, and further possible horrors which his timely coming had averted, was warm and eager in reinforcement of her husband's generous intentions.

But before that display of so much good will Don Pedro's face grew more and more forbidding. Sternly he shook his head.

'It is as I feared,' he said. 'Something which I cannot permit. If you insist, Don Sebastian, you will affront me. What I did yesterday was no more than was imposed upon me by my office. Neither thanks nor praise are due for a performance of bare duty. They are heroes only who, without thought of risk to themselves or concern for their own interests, perform deeds which are not within their duties. That, at least, is my conception. And, as I have said, to insist upon making a ballad of my conduct yesterday would be to affront me. You would not, I am sure, wish to do that, Don Sebastian.'

'Oh, but what modesty!' exclaimed the lady, joining her hands and casting up her eyes. 'How true it is that the great are always humble.'

Don Sebastian looked crestfallen. He sighed.

'It is an attitude worthy of a hero. True. But it disappoints me, my friend. It is a little return that I could make . . .'

'No return is due, Don Sebastian.' Don Pedro was forbiddingly peremptory. 'Let us speak of it no more, I beg of you.' He rose. 'I had better go aboard at once, to receive the Admiral's orders. I will inform him, in my own terms, of what has taken place here. And I can point to the gallows you are erecting on the beach for this pestilent Captain Blood. That will be most reassuring to his excellency.'

Of how reassuring it was Don Pedro brought news when towards noon he came ashore again, no longer in the borrowed, ill-fitting clothes, but arrayed once more in all the glories of a *grande* of Spain.

'The Marquis of Riconete asks me to inform you that since the Caribbean is happily delivered of the infamous Captain Blood, his excellency's mission in these waters is at an end, and nothing now prevents him from yielding to the urgency of returning to Spain at once. He has decided to convoy the plate ships across the ocean, and he begs you to instruct their captains to be ready to weigh anchor on the first of the ebb: this afternoon at three.'

Don Sebastian was aghast.

'But did you not tell him, sir, that it is impossible?'

Don Pedro shrugged. 'One does not argue with the Admiral of the Ocean-Sea.'

'But, my dear Don Pedro, more than half the crews are absent and the ships are without guns.'

'Be sure that I did not fail to inform his excellency of that. It merely annoyed him. He takes the view that since each ship carries hands enough to sail her, no more is necessary. The *Maria Gloriosa* is sufficiently armed to protect them.'

'He does not pause, then, to reflect what may happen should they become separated?'

'That also I pointed out. It made no impression. His excellency is of a high confidence.'

Don Sebastian blew out his cheeks.

'So! So! To be sure, it is his affair. And I thank God for it. The plate ships have brought trouble enough upon San Juan de Puerto Rico, and I'll be glad to see the last of them. But permit me to observe that your Admiral of the Ocean-Sea is a singularly rash man. It comes, I suppose, of being a royal favourite.'

Don Pedro's sly little smile suggested subtly complete agreement.

'It is understood, then, that you will give orders for the promptest victualling of the ships. His excellency must not be kept waiting, and, anyway, the ebb will not wait even for him.'

'Oh, perfectly,' said Don Sebastian. Irony exaggerated his submission. 'I will give the orders at once.'

'I will inform his excellency. He will be gratified. I take my leave, then, Don Sebastian.' They embraced. 'Believe me I shall long treasure the memory of our happy and profitable association. My homage to Doña Leocadia.'

'But will you not stay to see the hanging of Captain Blood? It is to take place at noon.'

'The Admiral expects me aboard at eight bells. I dare not keep him waiting.'

But on his way to the harbour, Captain Blood paused at the town gaol. By the officer in charge he was received with the honour due to the saviour of San Juan, and doors were unlocked at his bidding.

Beyond a yard in which the heavily ironed, dejected prisoners of yesterday's affray were herded, he came to a stone chamber lighted by a small window set high and heavily barred. In this dark, noisome hole sat the great buccaneer, hunched on a stool, his head in his manacled hands. He looked up as the door groaned on its hinges, and out of a livid face he glared at his visitor. He did not recognize his grimy opponent of yesterday in this elegant gentleman in black and silver, whose sedulously curled black periwig fell to his shoulders and who swung a gold-headed ebony cane as he advanced.

'Is it time?' he growled in his bad Spanish.

The apparent Castilian nobleman answered him in the English that is spoken in Ireland.

'Och, now, don't be impatient. Ye've still time to be making your soul, that is, if ye've a soul to make at all; still time to repent the nasty notion that led you into this imposture. I could forgive you the pretence that you are Captain Blood. There's a sort of compliment in that. But I can't be forgiving you the things you did in Cartagena: the wantonly murdered men, the violated women, the loathsome cruelties for cruelty's sake by which you slaked your evil lusts and dishonoured the name you assumed.'

The ruffian sneered. 'You talk like a canting parson sent to shrive me.'

'I talk like the man I am: the man whose name ye've befouled with the filth of your nature. I'll be leaving you to ponder, in the little time that's left you, the poetic justice by which mine is the hand that hangs you. For I am Captain Blood.'

A moment still he remained inscrutably surveying the doomed impostor whom amazement had rendered speechless; then turning on his heel, he went to rejoin the waiting Spanish officer.

Thence, past the gallows erected on the beach, he repaired to the waiting boat, and was pulled back to the white and gold flagship in the roads.

And so it befell that on that same day the false Captain Blood was hanged on the beach of San Juan de Puerto Rico, and the real Captain Blood sailed away for Tortuga in the *Maria Gloriosa,* or *Andalusian Lass,* convoying the richly laden plate ships, which had neither guns nor crews with which to offer resistance when the truth of their situation was later discovered to their captains.

3

The Demonstration

1

'FORTUNE,' CAPTAIN BLOOD was wont to say, 'detests a niggard. Her favours are reserved for the man who knows how to spend nobly and to stake boldly.'

Whether you hold him right or wrong in his opinion, it is at least beyond question that he never shrank from acting upon it. Instances of his prodigality are abundant in that record of his fortunes and hazards which Jeremy Pitt has left us, but none is more recklessly splendid than that supplied by his measures to defeat the West Indian policy of Monsieur de Louvois when it was threatening the great buccaneering brotherhood with extinction.

The Marquis de Louvois, who succeeded the great Colbert in the service of Louis XIV, was universally hated whilst he lived, and as universally lamented when he died. Than this conjunction of estimates there can be, I take it, no higher testimonial to the worth of a minister of state. Nothing was either too great or too small for Monsieur de Louvois's attention. Once he had set the machinery of state moving smoothly at home, he turned in his reorganizing lust to survey the French possessions in the Caribbean, where the activities of the buccaneers distressed his sense of orderliness.

Thither, in the King's twenty-four-gun ship the *Béarnais,* he despatched the Chevalier de Saintonges, an able, personable gentleman in the early thirties, who had earned a confidence which Monsieur de Louvois did not lightly bestow, and who bore now clear instructions upon how to proceed so as to put an end to the evil, as Monsieur de Louvois accounted it.

To Monsieur de Saintonges, whose circumstances in life were by no means opulent, this was to prove an unsuspected and Heaven-sent chance of fortune; for in the course of serving his King to the best of his ability, he found occasion, with an ability even greater, very abundantly to serve himself. During his sojourn in Martinique, which the events induced him to protract far beyond what was strictly necessary, he met, wooed at tropical speed, and married Madame de Veynac. This young and magnificently handsome widow of Hommaire de Veynac had inherited from her late husband those vast West Indian possessions which comprised nearly a third of the island of Martinique, with plantations of sugar, spices, and tobacco producing annual revenues that were nothing short of royal. Thus richly endowed, she came to the arms of the stately but rather impecunious Chevalier de Saintonges.

The Chevalier was too conscientious a man and too profoundly imbued with the sense of the importance of his mission to permit this marriage to be more than a splendid interlude in the diligent performance of the duties which had brought him to the New World. The nuptials having been celebrated in Saint-Pierre with all the pomp and luxury proper to the lady's importance, Monsieur de Saintonges resumed his task with the increased consequence which he derived from the happy change in his circumstances. He took his bride aboard the *Béarnais,* and sailed away from Saint-Pierre to complete his tour of inspection before setting a course for France and the full enjoyment of the fabulous wealth that was now his.

Dominica, Guadeloupe, and the Grenadines he had already visited, as well as Sainte-Croix, which properly speaking was the property, not of the French Crown, but of the French West India Company. The most important part of his mission, however, remained yet to be accomplished at Tortuga, that other property of the French West India Company, which had become the stronghold of those buccaneers, English, French, and Dutch, for whose extermination it was the Chevalier's duty to take order.

His confidence in his ability to succeed in this difficult matter had been materially augmented by the report that Peter Blood, the most dangerous and enterprising of all these filibusters, had lately been caught by the Spaniards and hanged at San Juan de Puerto Rico.

In calm but torrid August weather the *Béarnais* made a good passage and came to drop anchor in the Bay of Cayona, that rockbound harbour which Nature might have designed expressly to be a pirates' lair.

The Chevalier took his bride ashore with him, bestowing her in a chair expressly procured, for which his seamen opened a way through the heterogeneous crowd of Europeans, Negroes, Maroons, and Mulattoes of both sexes, who swarmed to view this great lady from the French ship. Two half-caste porters, all but naked, bore their chair with its precious cargo, whilst the rather pompous Monsieur de Saintonges, clad in the lightest of blue taffetas, cane in one hand and the hat with which he fanned himself in the other, stalked beside it, damning the heat, the flies, and the smells. A tall, florid man, already inclining slightly at this early age to embonpoint, he perspired profusely, and his head ran wet under his elaborate golden periwig.

Up the gentle acclivity of the main unpaved street of Cayona, with its fierce white glare of coral dust and its fringe of languid palms, he toiled to the blessed fragrant shade of the Governor's garden and eventually to the cool twilight of chambers from which the sun's ardour was excluded by green, slatted blinds. Here cool drinks, in which rum and limes and sugar-cane were skilfully compounded, accompanied the cordial welcome extended by the Governor and his two handsome daughters to these distinguished visitors.

But the heat in which Monsieur de Saintonges arrived was destined to be only temporarily allayed. Soon after Madame de Saintonges had been carried off by the Governor's daughters, a discussion ensued which reopened all the Chevalier's pores.

Monsieur d'Ogeron, who governed Tortuga on behalf of the French West India Company, had listened with a gravity increasing to gloom to the forcible expositions made by his visitor in the name of Monsieur de Louvois.

A slight, short, elegant man was this Monsieur d'Ogeron, who retained in this outlandish island of his rule something of the courtly airs of the great world from which he came, just as he surrounded himself in his house and its equipment with the elegancies proper to a French gentleman of birth. Only breeding and good manners enabled him now to dissemble his impatience. At the end of the Chevalier's blunt and pompous peroration, he fetched a sigh in which there was some weariness.

'I suspect,' he ventured, 'that Monsieur de Louvois is indifferently informed upon West Indian conditions.'

Monsieur de Saintonges was aghast at this hint of opposition. His sense of the importance and omniscience of Monsieur de Louvois was almost as high as his sense of his own possession of these qualities.

'I doubt, sir, if there are any conditions in the world upon which Monsieur le Marquis is not fully informed.'

Monsieur d'Ogeron's smile was gentle and courteous.

'All the world is, of course, aware of Monsieur de Louvois's high worth. But his excellency does not possess my own experience of these remotenesses, and this, I venture to think, lends some value to my opinion.'

By an impatient gesture the Chevalier waved aside the matter of Monsieur d'Ogeron's opinions.

'We lose sight of the point, I think. Suffer me to be quite blunt, sir. Tortuga is under the flag of France. Monsieur de Louvois takes the view, in which I venture to concur, that it is in the last degree improper . . . In short, that it is not to the honour of the flag of France that it should protect a horde of brigands.'

Monsieur d'Ogeron's gentle smile was still all deprecation.

'Sir, sir, it is not the flag of France that protects the

filibusters, but the filibusters that protect the flag of France.'

The tall, blond, rather imposing representative of the Crown came to his feet, as if to mark his indignation.

'Monsieur, that is an outrageous statement.'

The Governor's urbanity remained unimpaired.

'It is the fact that is outrageous, not the statement. Permit me to observe to you, monsieur, that a hundred and fify years ago, His Holiness the Pope bestowed upon Spain the New World of Columbus's discovery. Since then other nations, the French, the English, the Dutch, have paid less heed to that papal bull than Spain considers proper. They have attempted themselves to settle some of these lands; lands of which the Spaniards have never taken actual possession. Because Spain insists upon regarding this as a violation of her rights, the Caribbean for years has been a cockpit.

'These buccaneers themselves, whom you regard with such contempt, were originally peaceful hunters, cultivators, and traders. The Spaniards chased them out of Hispaniola, drove them, English and French, from Saint Christopher and the Dutch from Sainte-Croix, by ruthless massacres which did not spare even their women and children. In self-defence these men forsook their peaceful boucans, took arms, banded themselves together into a brotherhood, and hunted the Spaniard in their turn. That the Virgin Islands today belong to the English Crown is due to these Brethren of the Coast, as they call themselves, these buccaneers who took possession of those lands in the name of England. This very island of Tortuga, like the island of Sainte-Croix, came to belong to the French West India Company, and so to France, in the same way.

'You spoke, sir, of the protection of the French flag enjoyed by these buccaneers. There is here a confusion of ideas. If there were no buccaneers to hold the rapacity of Spain in check, I ask myself, Monsieur de Saintonges, if this voyage of yours would ever have been undertaken, for I doubt if there would have been any French possessions in the Caribbean to be visited.' He

paused to smile upon the blank amazement of his guest.
'I hope, monsieur, that I have said enough to justify the
opinion, which I take the liberty of holding in opposition
to that of Monsieur de Louvois, that the suppression of
the buccaneers might easily result in disaster to the
French West Indian colonies.'

At this point Monsieur de Saintonges exploded. As so
commonly happens it was actually a sense of the truth
underlying the Governor's argument that produced his
exasperation. The reckless terms of his rejoinder lead us
to doubt the wisdom of Monsieur de Louvois in choos-
ing him for an ambassador.

'You have said enough, monsieur . . . more than
enough to persuade me that a reluctance to forgo the
profits accruing to your Company and to yourself per-
sonally from the plunder marketed in Tortuga is rendering you negligent of the honour of France, upon which
this traffic is a stain.'

Monsieur d'Ogeron smiled no longer. Stricken in his
turn by the amount of truth in the Chevalier's accusation, he came to his feet suddenly, white with anger. But
a masterful, self-contained little man, he was without
any of the bluster of his tall visitor. His voice was as
cold as ice and very level.

'Such an assertion, monsieur, can be made to me only
sword in hand.'

Saintonges strode about the long room, and waved
his arms.

'That is of a piece with the rest! Preposterous! If
that's your humour, you had better send your cartel to
Monsieur de Louvois. I am but his mouthpiece. I have
said what I was charged to say, and what I would not
have said if I had found you reasonable. You are to
understand, monsieur, that I have not come all the way
from France to fight duels on behalf of the Crown, but
to explain the Crown's views and issue the Crown's
orders. If they appear distasteful to you, that is not my
affair. The orders I have for you are that Tortuga must
cease to be a haven for buccaneers. And that is all that
needs to be said.'

'God give me patience, sir!' cried Monsieur d'Ogeron in his distress. 'Will you be good enough to tell me at the same time how I am to enforce these orders?'

'Where is the difficulty? Close the market in which you receive the plunder. If you make an end of the traffic, the buccaneers will make an end of themselves.'

'How simple! But how very simple! And what if the buccaneers make an end of me and of this possession of the West India Company? What if they seize the island of Tortuga for themselves, which is no doubt what would happen? What, then, if you please, Monsieur de Saintonges?'

'The might of France will know how to enforce her rights.'

'Much obliged. Does the might of France realize how mighty it will have to be? Has Monsieur de Louvois any conception of the strength and organization of these buccaneers? Have you never, for instance, heard in France of Morgan's march on Panama? Is it realized that there are in all some five or six thousand of these men afloat, the most formidable sea-fighters the world has ever seen? If they were banded together by such a menace of extinction, they could assemble a navy of forty or fifty ships that would sweep the Caribbean from end to end.'

At last the Governor had succeeded in putting Monsieur de Saintonges out of countenance by these realities. For a moment the Chevalier stared chapfallen at his host. Then he rallied obstinately.

'Surely, sir, surely you exaggerate.'

'I exaggerate nothing. I desire you to understand that I am actuated by something more than the self-interest you so offensively attribute to me.'

'Monsieur de Louvois will regret, I am sure, the injustice of that assumption when I report to him fully, making clear what you have told me. For the rest, sir, however, you have your orders.'

'But surely, sir, you have been granted some discretion in the fulfilment of your mission. Finding things as

you do, as I have explained them, it seems to me that
you would do no disservice to the Crown in recommend-
ing to Monsieur de Louvois that until France is in a
position to place a navy in the Caribbean so as to protect her possessions, she would be well advised not to
disturb the existing state of things.'

The Chevalier merely stiffened further.

'That, monsieur, is not a recommendation that would
become me. You have the orders of Monsieur de Louvois, which are that this mart for the plunder of the
seas must at once be closed. I trust that you will enable
me to assure Monsieur de Louvois of your immediate
compliance.'

Monsieur d'Ogeron was in despair before the stupidity of this official intransigence.

'I must still protest, monsieur, that your description is
not a just one. No plunder comes here but the plunder
of Spain to compensate us for all the plunder we have
suffered and shall continue to suffer at the hands of the
gentlemen of Castile.'

'That, sir, is fantastic. There is peace between Spain
and France.'

'In the Caribbean, Monsieur de Saintonges, there is
never peace. If we abolish the buccaneers, we lay down
our arms and offer our throats to the knife. That is all.'

There were, however, no arguments that could move
Monsieur de Saintonges from the position he had taken
up. 'I must regard that as a personal opinion, more or
less coloured—suffer me to say it without offence—by
the interests of your Company and yourself. Anyway,
the orders are clear. You realize that you will neglect
them at your peril.'

'And also that I shall fulfil them at my peril,' said the
Governor, with a twist of the lips. He shrugged and
sighed. 'You place me, sir, between the sword and the
wall.'

'Do me the justice to understand that I discharge my
duty,' said the lofty Chevalier de Saintonges, and the
concession of those words was the only concession

Monsieur d'Ogeron could wring from his obstinate self-sufficiency.

2

Monsieur de Saintonges sailed away with his wife that same evening from Tortuga, setting a course for Port-au-Prince, where he desired to pay a call before finally steering for France and the opulent ease which he could now command there.

Admiring himself for the firmness with which he had resisted all the Governor of Tortuga's special pleading, he took Madame de Saintonges into his confidence in the matter, so that she, too, might admire him.

'That little trafficker in brigandage might have persuaded me from my duty if I had been less alert,' he laughed. 'But I am not easily deceived. That is why Monsieur de Louvois chose me for a mission of this importance. He knew the difficulties I should meet, and knew that I should not be duped by misrepresentations however specious.'

She was a tall, handsome, languorous lady, sloe-eyed, black-haired, with a skin like ivory and a bosom of Hebe. Her languishing eyes considered in awe and reverence this husband from the great world who was to open for her social gates in France that would have been closed against the wife of a mere planter, however rich. Yet for all her admiring confidence in his acumen, she ventured to wonder was he correct in regarding as purely self-interested the arguments which Monsieur d'Ogeron had presented. She had not spent her life in the West Indies without learning something of the predatoriness of Spain, although perhaps she had never until now suspected the extent to which the activities of the buccaneers might be keeping that predatoriness in check. Spain maintained a considerable fleet in the Caribbean, mainly for the purpose of guarding her settlements from filibustering raids. The suppression of the filibusters would render that fleet comparatively idle,

and in idleness there is no knowing to what devilry men
may turn, especially if they be Spaniards.

Thus, meekly, Madame de Saintonges to her adored
husband. But the adored husband, with the high spirit
that rendered him so adorable, refused to be shaken.

'In such an event, be sure that the King of France, my
master, will take order.'

Nevertheless, his mind was not quite at rest. His
wife's very submissive and tentative support of Monsieur d'Ogeron's argument had unsettled it again. It
was easy to gird at the self-interest of the Governor of
Tortuga, and to assign to it his dread of Spain. Monsieur
de Saintonges, because himself he had acquired a sudden and enormous interest in French West Indian possessions, began to ask himself whether, after all, he
might not have been too ready to believe that Monsieur
d'Ogeron had exaggerated.

And the Governor of Tortuga had not exaggerated.
However much his interests may have jumped with his
arguments, there can be no doubt whatever that these
were well founded. Because of this he could perceive
ahead of him no other course but to resign his office and
return at once to France, leaving Monsieur de Louvois
to work out the destinies of the French West Indies and
of Tortuga in his own fashion. It would be a desertion
of the interests of the West India Company. But if the
new minister's will prevailed, very soon the West India
Company would have no interests to protect.

The little governor spent a disturbed night, and slept
late on the following morning, to be eventually aroused
by gunfire.

The boom of cannon and the rattle of musketry were
so continuous that it took him some time to realize that
the din did not betoken an attack upon the harbour, but
a *feu-de-joie* such as the rocks of Cayona had never yet
echoed. The reason for it when he discovered it served
to dispel some part of his dejection. The report that
Peter Blood had been taken and hanged at San Juan de
Puerto Rico was being proved false by the arrival in
Cayona of Peter Blood himself. He had sailed into the

harbour aboard a captured Spanish vessel, the sometime *Maria Gloriosa*, lately the flagship of the Marquis of Riconete, the Admiral of the Ocean-Sea, trailing in her wake the two richly laden Spanish galleons, the plate ships taken at Puerto Rico.

The guns that thundered their salutes were the guns of Blood's own fleet of three ships, which had been refitting at Tortuga in his absence and aboard which during the past week all had been mourning and disorientation.

Rejoicing as fully as any of those jubilant buccaneers in this return from the dead of a man whom he, too, had mourned—for a real friendship existed between the Governor of Tortuga and the great captain—Monsieur d'Ogeron and his daughters prepared for Peter Blood a feast of welcome, to which the Governor brought some of those bottles 'from behind the faggots,' as he described the choice wines that he received from France.

The Captain came in great good-humour to the feast, and entertained them at table with an account of the queer adventure in Puerto Rico, which had ended in the hanging of a poor scoundrelly pretender to the name and fame of Captain Blood, and had enabled him to sail away unchallenged with the two plate ships that were now anchored in the harbour of Tortuga.

'I never made a richer haul, and I doubt if many richer have ever been made. Of the gold alone my own share must be a matter of twenty-five thousand pieces of eight, which I'll be depositing with you against bills of exchange on France. Then the peppers and spices in one of the galleons should be worth over a hundred thousand pieces to the West India Company. It awaits your valuation, my friend.'

But an announcement which should have increased the Governor's good-humour merely served to precipitate him visibly into the depths of gloom by reminding him of how the circumstances had altered. Sorrowfully he looked across the table at his guest, and sorrowfully he shook his head.

'All that is finished, my friend. I am under a cursed

interdict.' And forth in fullest detail came the tale of the
visit of the Chevalier de Saintonges with its curtailment
of Monsieur d'Ogeron's activities. 'So you see, my dear
Captain, the markets of the West India Company are
now closed to you.'

The keen, shaven, sunburned face in its frame of
black curls showed an angry consternation.

'Name of God! But didn't you tell this lackey from
court that . . .'

'There was nothing I did not tell him to which a man
of sense should have listened, no argument that I did
not present. To all that I had to say he wearied me with
insistence that he doubted if there were any conditions
in the world upon which Monsieur de Louvois is not informed. To the Chevalier de Saintonges there is no
god but Louvois and Saintonges is his prophet. So much
was plain. A consequential gentleman this Monsieur de
Saintonges, like all these court minions. Lately in Martinique he married the widow of Hommaire de Veynac.
That will make him one of the richest men in France.
You know the effect of great possessions on a self-
sufficient man.' Monsieur d'Ogeron spread his hands. 'It
is finished, my friend.'

But with this Captain Blood could not agree.

'That is to bend your head to the axe. Oh, no, no.
Defeat is not to be accepted so easily by men of our
strength.'

'For you, who dwell outside the law, all things are
possible. But for me . . . Here in Tortuga I represent the
law of France. I must serve and uphold it. And the law
has pronounced.'

'Had I arrived a day sooner the law might have been
made to pronounce differently.'

D'Ogeron was wistfully sardonic.

'You imagine, in spite of all that I have said, that you
could have persuaded this coxcomb of his folly?'

'There is nothing of which a man cannot be persuaded if the proper arguments are put before him in
the proper manner.'

'I tell you that I put before him all the arguments that exist.'

'No, no. You presented only those that occurred to you.'

'If you mean that I should have put a pistol to the head of this insufferable puppy . . .'

'Oh, my friend! That is not an argument. It is a constraint. We are all of us self-interested, and none are more so than those who, like this Chevalier de Saintonges, are ready to accuse others of that fault. An appeal to his interests might have been persuasive.'

'Perhaps. But what do I know of his interests?'

'What do you know of them? Oh, but think. Have you not yourself just told me that he lately married the widow of Hommaire de Veynac? That gives him great West Indian interests. You spoke vaguely and generally of Spanish raids upon the settlements of other nations. You should have been more particular. You should have dwelt upon the possibility of a raid upon wealthy Martinique. That would have given him to think. And now he's gone, and the chance is lost.'

But d'Ogeron would see no reason for sharing any regrets of that lost opportunity.

'His obstinacy would have prevented him from taking fright. He would not have listened. The last thing he said to me before he sailed for Port-au-Prince . . .'

'For Port-au-Prince!' ejaculated Captain Blood, to interrupt him. 'He's gone to Port-au-Prince?'

'That was his destination when he departed yesterday. It's his last port of call before he sails for France.'

'So, so!' The Captain was thoughtful. 'That means, then, that he will be returning by way of the Tortuga Channel?'

'Of course, since in the alternative he would have to sail round Hispaniola.'

'Now, glory be, I may not be too late, after all. Couldn't I intercept him as he returns and try my persuasive arts on him?'

'You'ld waste your time, Captain.'

'You make too sure. It's the great gift of persuasion I have. Sustain your hopes a while, my friend, until I put Monsieur de Saintonges to the test.'

But to raise from their nadir the hopes of Monsieur d'Ogeron something more was necessary than mere light-hearted assurances. It was with the sigh of an abiding despondency that he bade farewell that day to Captain Blood, and without confidence that he wished him luck in whatever he might adventure.

What form the adventure might take, Captain Blood himself did not yet know when he quitted the Governor's house and went aboard his own splendid forty-gun-ship the *Arabella,* which, ready for sea, fitted, armed, and victualled, had been standing idle during his late absence. But the thought he gave the matter was to such good purpose that late that same afternoon, with a definite plan conceived, he held a council of war in the great cabin, and assigned particular duties to his leading associates.

Hagthorpe and Dyke were to remain in Tortuga in charge of the treasure-ships. Wolverstone was given command of the Spanish Admiral's captured flagship the *Maria Gloriosa,* and was required to sail at once, with very special and detailed instructions. To Yberville, the French buccaneer who was associated with him, Blood entrusted the *Elizabeth,* with order to make ready to put to sea.

That same evening, at sunset, the *Arabella* was warped out of the swarm of lesser shipping that had collected about her anchorage. With Blood himself in command, with Pitt for sailing master and Ogle for master gunner, she set sail from Cayona, followed closely by the *Elizabeth.* The *Maria Gloriosa* was already hull down on the horizon.

Beating up against gentle easterly breezes, the two buccaneer ships, the *Arabella* and her consort, were off Point Palmish on the northern coast of Hispaniola by the following evening. Hereabouts, where the Tortuga Channel narrows to a mere five miles between Palmish and Portugal Point, Captain Blood decided to take up his station for what was to be done.

3

At about the time that the *Arabella* and the *Elizabeth* were casting anchor in that lonely cove on the northern coast of Hispaniola, the *Béarnais* was weighing at Port-au-Prince. The smells of the place offended the delicate nostrils of Madame de Saintonges, and on this account —since wives so well endowed are to be pampered— the Chevalier cut short his visit even at the cost of scamping the King's business. Glad to have set a term to this at last, with the serene conviction of having discharged his mission in a manner that must deserve the praise of Monsieur de Louvois, the Chevalier now turned his face towards France and his thoughts to lighter and more personal matters.

With a light wind abeam, the progress of the *Béarnais* was so slow that it took her twenty-four hours to round Cape Saint Nicholas at the western end of the Tortuga Channel; so that it was somewhere about sunset on the day following that of her departure from Port-au-Prince that she entered that narrow passage.

Monsieur de Saintonges at the time was lounging elegantly on the poop, beside a day-bed set under an awning of brown sail-cloth. On this day-bed reclined his handsome Créole wife. There was about this superbly proportioned lady, from the deep mellowness of her voice to the great pearls entwined in her glossy black hair, nothing that did not announce her opulence. It was enhanced at present by profound contentment in this marriage in which each party so perfectly complemented the other. She seemed to glow and swell with it as she lay there luxuriously, faintly waving her jewelled fan, her rich laugh so ready to pay homage to the wit with which her bridegroom sought to dazzle her.

Into this idyll stepped, more or less abruptly, and certainly intrusively, Monsieur Luzan, the captain of the *Béarnais,* a lean, brown, hook-nosed man something above the middle height, whose air and carriage were those of a soldier rather than a seaman. As he approached, he took the telescope from under his arm, and pointed aft with it.

'Yonder is something that is odd,' he said. And he held out the glass. 'Take a look, Chevalier.'

Monsieur de Saintonges rose slowly, and his eyes followed the indication. Some three miles to westward a sail was visible.

'A ship,' he said, and languidly accepted the proffered telescope. He stepped aside to the rail, whence the view was clearer and where he could find a support on which to steady his elbow.

Through the glass he beheld a big white vessel very high in the poop. She was veering northward, on a starboard tack against the easterly breeze, and so displayed a noble flank pierced for twenty-four guns, the ports gleaming gold against the white. From her main-topmast, above a mountain of snowy canvas, floated the red-and-gold banner of Castile, and above this a crucifix was mounted.

The Chevalier lowered the glass.

'A Spaniard,' was his casual comment. 'What oddness do you discover in her, Captain?'

'Oh, a Spaniard manifestly. But she was steering south when first we sighted her. A little later she veered into our wake and she crowded sail. That is what is odd. For the inference is that she decided to follow us.'

'What, then?'

'Just so. What, then?' He paused as if for a reply, then resumed. 'From the position of her flag she is an admiral's ship. You will have observed that she is of a heavy armament. She carries forty-eight guns besides stern- and fore-chasers.' Again he paused, finally to add with some force: 'When I am followed by a ship like that, I like to know the reason.'

Madame stirred languidly on her day-bed to an accompaniment of deep, rich laughter.

'Are you a man to start at shadows, Captain?'

'Invariably, when cast by a Spaniard, madame.' Luzan's tone was sharp. He was of a peppery temper, and this was stirred by the reflection upon his courage which he found implied in madame's question.

The Chevalier, disliking the tone, permitted himself some sarcasms where he would have been better employed in inquiring into the reasons for the captain's misgivings. Luzan departed in annoyance.

That night the wind dropped to the merest breath, and so slow was their progress that by the following dawn they were still some five or six miles to the west of Portugal Point and the exit of the straits. And daylight showed them the big Spanish ship ever at about the same distance astern. Uneasily and at length Captain Luzan scanned her once more, then passed his glass to his lieutenant.

'See what she can tell you.'

The lieutenant looked long, and whilst he looked he saw her making the addition of stunsails to the mountain of canvas that she already carried. This he announced to the captain at his elbow, and then, having scanned the pennant on her foretopmast, he was able to add the information that she was the flagship of the Spanish Admiral of the Ocean-Sea, the Marquis of Riconete.

That she should put out stunsails so as to catch the last possible ounce of the light airs increased the captain's suspicion that her aim was to overhaul him, and being imbued, as became an experienced seaman whilst in these waters, with a healthy mistrust of the intentions of all Spaniards, he took his decision. Crowding all possible sail, and as close-hauled as he dared run, he headed south for the shelter of one of the harbours of the northern coast of French Hispaniola. Thither this Spaniard, if she was indeed in pursuit, would hardly dare to follow him. If she did, she would certainly not venture to display hostility. The manoeuvre would also serve to apply a final test to her intentions.

The result supplied Luzan with almost immediate certainty. At once the great galleon was seen to veer in the same direction, actually thrusting her nose yet a point nearer to such wind as there was. It became as clear that she was in pursuit of the *Béarnais* as that the *Béarnais* would be cut off before ever she could reach the green coast that was now almost ahead of her, but still some four miles distant.

Madame de Saintonges, greatly incommoded in her cabin by the apparently quite unnecessary list to starboard, demanded impatiently to be informed by Heaven or Hell what might be amiss that morning with the fool who commanded the *Béarnais*. The uxorious Chevalier, in bed-gown and slippers, and with a hurriedly donned periwig, the curls of which hung like a row of tallow candles about his flushed countenance, made haste to go and ascertain.

He reeled along the almost perpendicular deck of the gangway to the ship's waist, and stood there bawling angrily for Luzan.

The captain appeared at the poop-rail to answer him with a curt account of his apprehensions.

'Are you still under that absurd persuasion?' quoth Monsieur de Saintonges. 'Absurd. Why should a Spaniard be in pursuit of us?'

'It will be better to continue to ask ourselves that question than to wait to discover the answer,' snapped Luzan, thus, by his lack of deference, increasing the Chevalier's annoyance.

'But it is imbecile, this!' raved Saintonges. 'To run away from nothing! And it is infamous to discompose Madame de Saintonges by fears so infantile.'

Luzan's patience completely left him.

'She'll be infinitely more discomposed,' he sneered, 'if these infantile fears are realized.' And he added bluntly: 'Madame de Saintonges is a handsome woman, and Spaniards are Spaniards.'

A shrill exclamation was his answer, to announce that madame herself had now emerged from the companionway. She was in a state of undress that barely preserved the decencies; for without waiting to cast more than a wrap over her night-rail, and with a mane of lustrous black hair like a cloak about her splendid shoulders, she had come to ascertain for herself what might be happening.

Luzan's remarks, overheard as she was stepping into the ship's waist, brought upon him now a torrent of shrill abuse, in the course of which he heard himself described as a paltry coward and a low, coarse wretch. And before she had done, the Chevalier was adding his voice to hers.

'You are mad, sir! Mad! What can we possibly have to fear from a Spanish ship, a King's ship, you tell me, an Admiral? We fly the flag of France, and Spain is not at war with France.'

Luzan controlled himself to answer as quietly as he might.

'In these waters, sir, it is impossible to say with whom Spain may be at war. Spain is persuaded that God created the Americas especially for her delight. I have been telling you this ever since we entered the Caribbean.'

The Chevalier remembered not only this, but also that from someone else he had lately heard expressions very similar. Madame, however, was distracting his attention.

'The man's wits are turned by panic!' she railed in furious contempt. 'It is terrible that such a man should be entrusted with a ship. He would be better fitted to command a kitchen battery.'

Heaven alone knows what might have been the answer to that insult and what the consequences of it if at that very moment the boom of a gun had not come to save Luzan the trouble of a reply, and abruptly to change the scene and the tempers of the actors.

'Righteous Heaven!' screamed madame, and 'Ventre-dieu!' swore her husband.

The lady clutched her bosom. The Chevalier, with a face of chalk, put an arm protectingly about her. From the poop the captain whom they had so freely accused of cowardice laughed outright with a well-savoured malice.

'You are answered, madame. And you, sir. Another

time perhaps you will reflect before you call my fears infantile and my conduct imbecile.'

With that he turned his back upon them, so that he might speak to the lieutenant who had hastened to his elbow. He bawled an order. It was instantly followed by the whistle of the boatswain's pipe, and in the waist about Saintonges and his bride there was a sudden jostling stir as the hands came pouring from their quarters to be marshalled for whatever the captain might require of them. Aloft there was another kind of activity. Men were swarming the ratlines and spreading nets whose purpose was to catch any spars that might be brought down in the course of action.

A second gun boomed from the Spaniard and then a third; after that there was a pause, and then they were saluted by what sounded like the thunder of a whole broadside.

The Chevalier lowered his white and shaking wife, whose knees had suddenly turned to water, to a seat on the hatch-coaming. He was futilely profane in his distress.

From the rail Luzan, taking pity on them, and entirely unruffled, uttered what he believed to be reassurance.

'At present she is burning powder to no purpose. Mere Spanish bombast. She'll come within range before I fire a shot. My gunners have their orders.'

But, far from reassuring them, this was merely to increase the Chevalier's fury and distress.

'God of my life! Return her fire? You mustn't think of it. You can't deliver battle.'

'Can't I? You shall see.'

'But you cannot go into action with Madame de Saintonges on board.'

'You want to laugh!' said Luzan. 'If I had the Queen of France on board, I must still fight my ship. And I have no choice, pray observe. We are being overhauled too fast to make harbour in time. And how do I know that we should be safe even then?'

The Chevalier stamped in rage.

'But they are brigands, then, these Spaniards?'

There was another roar of artillery at closer quarters now, which, if still not close enough for damage, was close enough to increase the panic of Monsieur and Madame de Saintonges.

The captain was no longer heeding them. His lieutenant had clutched his arm, and was pointing westward. Luzan with the telescope to his eye was following that indication.

A mile or so off on their starboard beam, midway between the *Béarnais* and the Spanish Admiral, a big red forty-gun ship under full sail was creeping into view round a headland of the Hispaniola coast. Close in her wake came a second ship of an armament only a little less powerful. They flew no flag, and it was in increasing apprehension that Luzan watched their movements, wondering were they fresh assailants. To his almost incredulous relief, he saw them veer to larboard, heading in the direction of the Spaniard, half-hidden still in the smoke of her last cannonade which that morning's gentle airs were slow to disperse.

Light though the wind might be, the newcomers had the advantage of it, and with the weather gauge of the Spaniard they advanced upon him, like hawks stooping to a heron, opening fire with their fore-chasers as they went.

Through a veil of rising smoke the Spaniard could be discerned easing up to receive them; then a half-dozen guns volleyed from her flank, and she was again lost to view in the billowing white clouds they had belched. But she seemed to have fired wildly in her excessive haste, for the red ship and her consort held steadily for some moments on their course, evidently unimpaired, then swung to starboard, and delivered each an answering broadside at the Spaniard.

By now, under Luzan's directions, and despite the protests of Monsieur Saintonges, the *Béarnais,* too, had eased up until she stood with idly flapping sails, suddenly changed from actor to spectator in this drama of the seas.

'Why do you pause, sir?' cried Saintonges. 'Keep to your course! Take advantage of this check to make that harbour.'

'Whilst others fight my battles for me?'

'You have a lady on board,' Saintonges raged at him. 'Madame de Saintonges must be placed in safety.'

'She is in no danger at present. And we may be needed. Awhile ago you accused me of cowardice. Now you would persuade me to become a coward. For the sake of Madame de Saintonges I will not go into battle save in the last extremity. But for that last extremity I must stand prepared.'

He was so grimly firm that Saintonges dared insist no further. Instead, setting his hopes upon those Heaven-sent rescuers, he stood on the hatch-coaming, and from that elevation sought to follow the fortunes of the battle which was roaring away to westward. But there was nothing to be seen now save a great curtain of smoke, like a vast-spreading, deepening cloud that hung low over the sea and extended for perhaps two miles in the sluggish air. From somewhere within the heart of it they continued for a while to hear the thunder of the guns. Then came a spell of silence, and after a time on the southern edge of the cloud two ships appeared that were at first as the wraiths of ships. Gradually rigging and hulls assumed definition as the smoke rolled away from them, and at about the same time the heart of the cloud began to assume a rosy tint, deepening swiftly to orange, until through the thinning smoke it was seen to proceed from the flames of a ship on fire.

From the poop-rail, Luzan's announcement brought relief at last to the Chevalier.

'The Spanish Admiral is burning. It is the end of her.'

4

One of the two ships responsible for the destruction of the Spanish galleon remained hove-to on the scene of action, her boats lowered and ranging the waters in her neighbourhood. This Luzan made out through his telescope. The other and larger vessel, emerging from that brief decisive engagement without visible scars, headed eastward, and came beating up against the wind towards the *Béarnais,* her red hull and gilded beakhead aglow in the morning sunshine. Still she displayed no flag, and this circumstance renewed in Monsieur de Saintonges the apprehensions which the issue of the battle had allayed.

With his lady, still in her half-clad condition, he was now on the poop at Luzan's side, and to the captain he put the question was it prudent to remain hove-to whilst this ship of undeclared nationality advanced upon them.

'But hasn't she proved a friend? A friend in need?' said the captain.

Madame de Saintonges had not yet forgiven Luzan his plain speaking. Out of her hostility she answered him.

'You assume too much. All that we really know is that she proved an enemy to that Spanish ship. How do you know that these are not pirates to whom every ship is a prey? How do we know that since fire has robbed them of their Spanish prize, they may not be intent now upon compensating themselves at our expense?'

Luzan looked at her without affection.

'There is one thing I know,' said he tartly. 'Her sailing powers are as much in excess of our own as her armament. It would avail us little to turn a craven tail if she means to overtake us. And there is another thing. If they meant us mischief, one of those ships would not have remained behind. The two of them would be heading for us. So we need not fear to do what courtesy dictates.'

This argument was reassuring, and so the *Béarnais* waited whilst in the breeze that was freshening now the stranger came rippling forward over the sunlit water. At a distance of less than a quarter of a mile she hove-to. A boat was lowered to the calm sea and came speeding with flash of yellow oars towards the *Béarnais.* Out of her a tall man climbed the Jacob's-ladder of the French vessel, and came to stand upon the poop in an elegance of black-and-silver, from which you might suppose him to have come straight from Versailles or the Alameda rather than from the deck of a ship in action.

To the group that received him there—Monsieur de Saintonges and his wife in their disarray, with Luzan and his lieutenant—this stately gentleman bowed until the curls of his periwig met across his square chin, whilst the claret feather in his doffed hat swept the deck.

'I come,' he announced in fairly fluent French, 'to bear and receive felicitations, and to assure myself before sailing away that you are in no need of further assistance and that you suffered no damage before we had the honour to intervene and dispose of that Spanish brigand who was troubling you.'

Such gallant courtesy completely won them, especially the lady. They reassured him on their own score and were solicitous as to what hurts he might have taken in the fight, for all that none were manifest.

Of these he made light. He had suffered some damage on the larboard quarter, which they could not see, but so slight as not to be worth remarking, whilst his men had taken scarcely a scratch. The fight, he explained, had been as brief as, in one sense, it was regrettable. He had hoped to make a prize of that fine galleon. But before he could close with her, a shot had found and fired her powder magazine, and so the little affair ended almost before it was well begun. He had picked up most of her crew, and his consort was still at that work of rescue.

'As for the flagship of the Admiral of the Ocean-Sea, you see what's left of her, and very soon you will not see even that.'

They carried off this airy, elegant preserver to the great cabin, and in the wine of France they pledged his opportuneness and the victory which had rescued them from ills unnameable. Yet throughout there was from black-and-silver no hint of his identity or nationality, although this they guessed from his accent to be English. Saintonges, at last, approached the matter obliquely.

'You fly no flag, sir,' he said, when they had drunk.

The swarthy gentleman laughed. He conveyed the impression that laughter came to him readily.

'Sir, to be frank with you, I am of those who fly any flag that the occasion may demand. It might have been reassuring if I had approached you under French colours. But in the stress of the hour I gave no thought to it. You could hardly mistake me for a foe.'

'Of those that fly no flag?' the Chevalier echoed, staring bewilderment.

'Just so.' And airily he continued: 'At present I am on my way to Tortuga, and in haste. I am to assemble men and ships for an expedition to Martinique.'

It was the lady's turn to grow round-eyed.

'To Martinique?' She seemed suddenly a little out of breath. 'An expedition to Martinique? An expedition? But to what end?'

Her intervention had the apparent effect of taking him by surprise. He looked up, raising his brows. He smiled a little, and his answer had the tone of humouring her.

'There is a possibility—I will put it no higher—that Spain may be fitting out a squadron for a raid upon Saint-Pierre. The loss of the Admiral which I have left in flames out yonder may delay their preparations, and so give us more time. It is what I hope.'

Rounder still grew her dark eyes, paler her cheeks. Her deep bosom was heaving now in tumult.

'Do you say that Spaniards propose a raid upon Martinique? Upon Martinique?'

And the Chevalier, in an excitement scarcely less marked than his wife's, added at once:

'Impossible, sir. Your information must be at fault. God of my life! That would be an act of war. And France and Spain are at peace.'

The dark brows of their preserver were raised again as if in amusement at their simplicity.

'An act of war. Perhaps. But was it not an act of war for that Spanish ship to fire upon the French flag this morning? Would the peace that prevails in Europe have availed you in the West Indies if you had been sunk?'

'An account—a strict account would have been asked of Spain.'

'And it would have been rendered, not a doubt. With apologies of the fullest and some lying tales of a misunderstanding. But would that have set your ship afloat again if she had been sunk this morning, or restored you to life so that you might expose the lies by which Spanish men of state would cover the misdeed? Has this not happened, too, and often, when Spain has raided the settlements of other nations?'

'But not of late, sir,' Saintonges retorted.

Black-and-silver shrugged.

'Perhaps that is just the reason why the Spaniards in the Caribbean grow restive.'

And by that answer Monsieur de Saintonges was silenced, bewildered.

'But Martinique!' wailed the lady.

Black-and-silver shrugged expressively.

'The Spaniards call it Martinico, madame. You are to remember that Spain believes that God created the New World especially for her profit, and that the Divine Will approves her resentment of all interlopers.'

'Isn't that just what I told you, Chevalier?' said Luzan. 'Almost my own words to you this morning when you would not believe there could be danger from a Spanish ship.'

There was an approving gleam from the bright blue eyes of the swarthy stranger as they rested on the French captain.

'So, so. Yes. It is hard to believe. But you have now the proof of it, I think, that in these waters, as in the islands of the Caribbean Sea, Spain respects no flag but her own unless force is present to compel respect. The settlers of every other nation have experiencd in turn the Spaniard's resentment of their presence here. It expresses itself in devastating raids, in rapine, and in massacre. I need not enumerate instances. They will be present in your mind. If today it should happen, indeed, to be the turn of Martinico, we can but wonder that it should not have come before. For that is an island worth plundering and possessing, and France maintains no force in the West Indies that is adequate to restrain these *conquistadores*. Fortunately we still exist. If it were not for us . . .'

'For you?' Saintonges interrupted him, his voice suddenly sharp. 'You exist, you say. Of whom do you speak, sir? Who are you?'

The question seemed to take the stranger by surprise. He stared, expressionless, for a moment; then his answer, for all that it confirmed the suspicions of the Chevalier and the convictions of Luzan, was nevertheless as a thunderbolt to Saintonges.

'I speak of the Brethren of the Coast, of course. The buccaneers, sir.' And he added, almost it seemed with a sort of pride: 'I am Captain Blood.'

Blankly, his jaw fallen, Saintonges looked across the table into that dark, smiling face of the redoubtable fili-buster who had been reported dead.

To be faithful to his mission he should place this man in irons and carry him a prisoner to France. But not only would that in the circumstances of the moment be an act of blackest ingratitude, it would be rendered im-possible by the presence at hand of two heavily armed buccaneer ships. Moreover, in the light so suddenly vouchsafed to him, Monsieur de Saintonges perceived that it would be an act of grossest folly. He considered what had happened that morning: the direct and very disturbing evidence of Spain's indiscriminate predatori-ness; the evidence of a buccaneer activity which he could not now regard as other than salutary, supplied by that burning ship a couple of miles away; the further evidence of one and the other contained in this news of an impending Spanish raid on Martinique and the in-tended buccaneer intervention to save it where France had not the means at hand. Considering all this—and the Martinique business touched him so closely and per-sonally that from being perhaps the richest man in France, he might find himself as a result of it no better

than he had been before this voyage—it leapt to the eye
that for once, at least, the omniscient Monsier de Louvois had been at fault. So clear was it and so demon-
strable that Saintonges began to conceive it his duty to
shoulder the burden of that demonstration.

Something of all these considerations and emotions
quivered in the hoarse voice in which, still staring blankly at Captain Blood, he ejaculated:

'You are that brigand of the sea!'

Blood displayed no resentment. He smiled.

'Oh, but a benevolent brigand, as you perceive.
Benevolent, that is, to all but Spain.'

Madame de Saintonges swung in a breathless excitement to her husband, clutching his arm. In the movement the wrap slipped from her shoulders, so that still
more of her opulent charms became revealed. But this
went unheeded by her. In such an hour of crisis modesty
became a negligible matter.

'Charles, what will you do?'

'Do?' said he dully.

'The orders you left in Tortuga may mean ruin to
me, and . . .'

He raised a hand to stem this betrayal of self-interest.
In whatever might have to be done, of course, no interest but the interest of his master the King of France
must be permitted to sway him.

'I see, my dear. I see. Duty becomes plain. We have
received a valuable lesson this morning. Fortunately before it is too late.'

She drew a deep breath of relief, and swung excitedly,
anxiously, to Captain Blood.

'You have no doubt in your mind, sir, that your buccaneers can ensure the safety of Martinique?'

'None, madame.' His tone was of a hard confidence.
'The Bay of Saint-Pierre will prove a mousetrap for the
Spaniards if they are so rash as to sail into it. I shall
know what is to do. And the plunder of their ships
alone will richly defray the costs of the expedition.'

And then Saintonges laughed.

'Ah, yes,' said he. 'The plunder, to be sure. I understand. The ships of Spain are a rich prey, when all is said. Oh, I do not sneer, sir. I hope I am not so ungenerous.'

'I could not suppose it, sir,' said Captain Blood. He pushed back his chair, and rose. 'I will be taking my leave. The breeze is freshening and I should seize the advantage. If it holds, I shall be in Tortuga this evening.'

He stood, inclined a little, before Madame de Saintonges, awaiting the proffer of her hand, when the Chevalier took him by the shoulder.

'A moment yet, sir. Keep madame company whilst I write a letter which you shall carry for me to the Governor of Tortuga.'

'A letter!' Captain Blood assumed astonishment. 'To commend this poor exploit of ours? Sir, sir, never be at so much trouble.'

Monsieur de Saintonges was for a moment ill-at-ease.

'It . . . it has a further purpose,' he said at last.

'Ah! If it is to serve some purpose of your own, that is another matter. Pray command me.'

5

In the faithful discharge of that courier's office Captain Blood laid the letter from the Chevalier de Saintonges on the evening of that same day before the Governor of Tortuga, without any word of explanation.

'From the Chevalier de Saintonges, you say?' Monsieur d'Ogeron was frowning thoughtfully. 'To what purpose?'

'I could guess,' said Captain Blood. 'But why should I, when the letter is in your hands? Read it, and we shall know.'

'In what circumstances did you obtain this letter?'

'Read it. It may tell you, and so save my breath.'

D'Ogeron broke the seal and spread the sheet. With knitted brows he read the formal retraction by the representative of the Crown of France of the orders left with

the Governor of Tortuga for the cessation of all traffic
with the buccaneers. Monsieur d'Ogeron was required
to continue relations with them as heretofore pending
fresh instructions from France. And the Chevalier added
the conviction that these instructions when and if they
came would nowise change the existing order of things.
He was confident that, when he had fully laid before the
Marquis de Louvois the demonstration he had received
of the conditions prevailing in the West Indies, his excellency would be persuaded of the inexpediency at
present of enforcing his decrees against the buccaneers.

Monsiur d'Ogeron blew out his cheeks.

'But will you tell me, then, how you worked this
miracle with that obstinate numbskull?'

'Every argument depends, as I said to you, upon the
manner of its presentation. You and I both said the
same thing to the Chevalier de Saintonges. But you said
it in words. I said it chiefly in action. Knowing that fools
learn only by experience, I supplied experience for him.
It was thus.' And he rendered a full account of that
early morning sea-fight off the northern coast of Hispaniola.

The Governor listened, stroking his chin.

'Yes,' he said slowly, when the tale was done. 'Yes.
That would be persuasive. And to scare him with this
bogey of a raid on Martinique and the probable loss of
his newfound wealth was well conceived. But don't you
flatter yourself a little, my friend, on the score of your
shrewdness? Are you forgetting how amazingly fortunate it was for you that in such a place and at such a
time a Spanish galleon should have had the temerity to
attack the *Béarnais*? Amazingly fortunate! It fits your
astounding luck most oddly!'

'Most oddly, as you say,' Blood solemnly agreed.

'What ship was this you burnt and sank? And what
fool commanded her? Do you know?'

'Oh, yes. The *Maria Gloriosa,* the flagship of the
Marquis of Riconete, the Spanish Admiral of the Ocean-
Sea.'

D'Ogeron looked up sharply.

'The *Maria Gloriosa?* What are you telling me? Why, you captured her yourself at San Domingo and came back here in her when you brought the treasure-ships.'

'Just so. And, therefore, I had her in hand for this little demonstration of Spanish turpitude and buccaneer prowess. She sailed with Wolverstone in command and just enough hands to work her and to man the half-dozen guns I spared her for the sacrifice.'

'God save us! Do you tell me, then, that it was all a comedy?'

'Mostly played behind a curtain of the smoke of battle. It was a very dense curtain. We supplied an abundance of smoke from guns loaded with powder only, and the light airs assisted us. Wolverstone set fire to the ship at the height of the supposed battle, and under cover of that friendly smoke came aboard the *Arabella* with his crew.'

The Governor continued to glare amazement.

'And you tell me that this was convincing?'

'That it was convincing, no. That it convinced.'

'And you deliberately—deliberately burnt that splendid Spanish ship!'

'That is what convinced. Merely to have driven her off might not have done so.'

'But the waste! Oh, my God, the waste!'

'Do you complain? Will you be cheeseparing? Do you think that it is by economies that great enterprises are carried through? Look at the letter in your hand again. It amounts to a government charter for a traffic against which there was a government decree. Do you think such things can be obtained by fine phrases? You tried them, and you know what came of it.' He slapped the little governor on the shoulder. 'Let's come to business. For now I shall be able to sell you my spices, and I warn you that I shall expect a good price for them: the price of three Spanish ships at least.'

4

The Deliverance

1

FOR A YEAR and more after his escape from Barbados with Peter Blood, it was the abiding sorrow of Nathaniel Hagthorpe, that West Country gentleman whom the force of adversity had made a buccaneer, that his younger brother Tom should still continue in the enslaved captivity from which himself he had won free.

Both these brothers had been out with Monmouth, and being taken after Sedgemoor, both had been sentenced to be hanged for their share in that rebellion. Then came the harsh commutation of the sentence which doomed them to slavery in the plantations, and with a shipload of other rebels-convict they had been sent out to Barbados and there had passed into the possession of the brutal Colonel Bishop. But by the time that Blood had come to organize the escape of himself and his fellows from that island, Tom Hagthorpe was no longer there.

Colonel Sir James Court, who was deputy in Nevis for the Governor of the Leeward Islands, had come on a visit to Bishop in Barbados, and had brought with him his young wife. She was a dainty, wilful piece of mischief, too young by far to have mated with so elderly a man, and, having been raised by her marriage to a station above that into which she had been born, she was the more insistent upon her ladyhood and of exactions and pretensions at which a duchess might have paused.

Newly arrived in the West Indies, she was resentfully

slow to adapt herself to some of the necessities of her environment, and among her pretensions arising out of this was the lack of a white groom to attend her when she rode abroad. It did not seem fitting to her that a person of her rank should be accompanied on those occasions by what she contemptuously termed a greasy blackamoor. Nevis, however, could offer her no other, fume as she might. Although by far the most important slave-mart in the West Indies, it imported this human merchandise only from Africa. Because of this, it had been omitted by the Secretary of State at home from the list of islands to which contingents of the West Country rebels had been shipped. Lady Court had a notion that this might be repaired in the course of that visit to Barbados, and it was Tom Hagthorpe's misfortune that her questing eyes should have alighted admiringly upon his clean-limbed almost stripling grace when she beheld him at work, half-naked, among Colonel Bishop's golden sugar-cane. She marked him for her own, and thereafter gave Sir James no peace until he had bought the slave from the planter who owned him. Bishop made no difficulty about the sale. To him one slave was much as another, and there was a delicacy about this particular lad which made him of indifferent value in a plantation and easily replaced.

Whilst the separation from his brother was a grief to Tom, yet at first the brothers were so little conscious of his misfortune that they welcomed this deliverance from the lash of the overseer; and, although a gentleman born, yet so abjectly was he fallen that they regarded it as a sort of promotion that he should go to Nevis to be a groom to the Colonel's lady. Therefore Nat Hagthorpe, taking comfort in the assurance of the lad's improved condition, did not grievously bewail his departure from Barbados until after his own escape, when the thought of his brother's continuing slavery was an abiding source of bitterness.

Tom Hagthorpe's confidence that at least he would gain by the change of owners and find himself in less

uneasy circumstances seems soon to have proved an il-
lusion. We are without absolute knowledge of how this
came about. But what we know of the lady, as will presently be disclosed, justifies a suspicion that she may
have exercised in vain the witchery of her long narrow
eyes on that comely lad; in short, that he played Joseph
to her Madam Potiphar, and thereby so enraged her
that she refused to have him continue in attendance. He
was clumsy, she complained, ill-mannered, and disposed
to insolence.

'I warned you,' said Sir James a little wearily, for her
exactions constantly multiplying were growing burden-
some, 'that he was born a gentleman, and must naturally resent his degradation. Better to have left him in the
plantations.'

'You can send him back to them,' she answered. 'For
I've done with the rascal.'

And so, deposed from the office for which he had
been acquired, he went to toil again at sugar-cane under
overseers no whit less brutal than Bishop's and was
given for associates a gang of gaol-birds, thieves, and
sharpers lately shipped from England.

Of this, of course, his brother had no knowledge, or
he must have been visited by a deeper dejection on
Tom's behalf and a fiercer impatience to see him delivered from captivity. For that was an object constantly
before Nat Hagthorpe, one that he constantly urged
upon Peter Blood.

'Will you be patient now?' the Captain would answer
him, himself driven to the verge of impatience by this
reiteration of an almost impossible demand. 'If Nevis
were a Spanish settlement, we could set about it without ceremony. But we haven't come yet to the point of
making war on English ships and English lands. That
would entirely ruin our prospects.'

'Prospects? What prospects have we?' growled Hagthorpe. 'We're outlawed, or aren't we?'

'Maybe, maybe. But we discriminate by being the
enemy of Spain alone. We're not *hostis humani generis*

yet, and until we become that, we need not abandon hope, like others of our kind, that one day this outlawry will be lifted. I'll not be putting that in jeopardy by a landing in force on Nevis, not even to save your brother, Nat.'

'Is he to languish there until he dies, then?'

'No, no. I'll find the way. Be sure I'll find it. But we'ld be wise to wait a while.'

'For what?'

'For Chance. It's a great faith I have in the lady. She's obliged me more than once, so she has; and she'll maybe oblige me again. But she's not a lady you can drive. Just put your faith in her, Nat, as I do.'

And in the end he was shown to be justified of that faith. The Chance upon which he depended came with unexpected suddenness to his assistance just after the affair of San Juan de Puerto Rico. The news that Captain Blood had been caught by the Spaniards and had expiated his misdeeds on a gallows on the beach of San Juan had swept like a hurricane across the Caribbean, from Hispaniola to the Main. In every Spanish settlement there was exultation over the hanging of the most formidable agent of restraint upon Spain's fierce predatoriness that had ever sailed the seas. For the same reason there was much secret, unavowed regret among the English and French colonists, by whom the buccaneers were, at least tacitly, encouraged.

Before very long it must come to be discovered that the treasure-ships which had sailed from San Juan under the convoy of the flagship of the Admiral of the Ocean-Sea had cast anchor, not in Cadiz Bay, but in the harbour of Tortuga, and that it was not the Admiral of the Ocean-Sea, but Captain Blood himself, who had commanded the flagship at the very time when his body could be seen dangling from that gallows on the beach. But until the discovery came, Captain Blood was concerned, like a wise opportunist, to profit by the authoritative report of his demise. He realized that there was no time to be lost if he would take full advantage of the present relaxation of vigilance throughout New Spain, and so he set out from the buccaneer stronghold of Tortuga on a projected descent upon the Main.

He took the seas in the *Arabella,* but she bore a broad white stripe painted along her water-line so as to dissemble her red hull, and on her counter the name displayed was now *Mary of Modena,* so as to supply an ultra-Stuart English antidote to her powerful, shapely Spanish lines. With the white, blue, and red of the Union flag at her maintruck, she put in at Saint Thomas, ostensibly for wood and water, actually to see what might be picked up. What she picked up was Mr. Geoffrey Court, who came to supply the Chance for which Nathaniel Hagthorpe had prayed and Captain Blood had confidently waited.

2

Over the emerald water that sparkled in the morning sunlight, in a boat rowed by four moistly gleaming Negroes, came Mr. Geoffrey Court, a consequential gentleman in a golden periwig and a brave suit of mauve taffetas with silver buttonholes.

Whilst the Negroes steadied the boat against the great hull, he climbed the accommodation-ladder in the prow, and stepped aboard fanning himself with his plumed hat, inviting Heaven to rot him if he could support this abominable heat, and peremptorily demanding the master of this pestilential vessel.

The adjective was merely a part of his habitual and limited rhetoric. For the deck on which he stood was scrubbed clean as a trencher; the brass of the scuttle-butts and the swivel-guns on the poop-rail gleamed like polished gold; the muskets in the rack about the mainmast could not have been more orderly or better furbished had this been a King's ship; and all the gear was stowed as daintily as in a lady's chamber.

The men lounging on the forecastle and in the waist,

few of them wearing more than a cotton shirt and a pair of loose calico drawers, observed the gentleman's arrogance with a mild but undisguised amusement to which he was happily blind.

A Negro steward led him by a dark gangway to the main cabin astern, which surprised him by its space and the luxury of its appointments. Here, at a table spread with snowy napery on which crystal and silver sparkled, sat three men, and one of these, spare and commanding of height, very elegant in black-and-silver, his sunburned hawk face framed in the flowing curls of a black periwig, rose to receive the visitor. The other two, who remained seated, if less imposing were yet of engaging aspect. They were Jeremy Pitt, the shipmaster, young and fair and slight of build, and Nathaniel Hagthorpe, older and broader and of a graver countenance.

Our gentleman in mauve lost none of his assurance under the calm survey to which those three pairs of eyes subjected him. His self-sufficiency proclaimed itself in the tone in which he desired to be informed whither the *Mary of Modena* might be bound. That he supplied a reason for the question seemed on his part a mere condescension.

'My name is Court. Geoffrey Court, to serve you, sir. I am in haste to reach Nevis, where my cousin commands.'

The announcement made something of a sensation upon his audience. It took the breaths of the three men before him, and from Hagthorpe came a gasping 'God save us!' whilst his sudden pallor must have been apparent even with his face in shadow, for he sat with the tall stern windows at his back. Mr. Court, however, was too much engrossed in himself to pay heed to changes in the aspect of another. He desired to impress them with his consequence.

'I am cousin to Sir James Court, who is Deputy in Nevis for the Governor of the Leeward Islands. You will have heard of him, of course.'

'Of course,' said Blood.

Hagthorpe's impatience was not content to wait.

'And you want us to carry you to Nevis?' he cried, out of breath, in an eagerness that would have been noticed by any man less obtuse.

'If your course lies anywhere in that direction. It's this way with me: I came out from home, may I perish, on a plaguey half-rotten ship that met foul weather and all but went to pieces under it. Her seams opened under the strain, and she was leaking like a colander when we ran in here for safety. You can see her at anchor yonder. May I rot if she'll ever be fit to take the seas again. The most cursed luck it was to have sailed in such a worm-eaten washtub.'

'And you're in haste to get to Nevis?' quoth Blood.

'In desperate haste, may I burn. I've been expected there this month past.'

It was Hagthorpe who answered him in a voice hoarse with emotion.

'Odslife, but you're singularly in luck, sir. For Nevis is our next port of call.'

'Stab me! And is that so?'

There was a grim smile on Blood's dark face.

'It's a strange chance, so it is,' he said. 'We weigh at eight bells, and if this wind holds it's tomorrow morning we'll be dropping anchor at Charlestown.'

'Nothing, then, could be more fortunate. Nothing, may I perish.' The florid countenance was all delight. 'Fate owes me something for the discomforts I have borne. By your leave, I'll fetch my portmantles at once.' Magnificently he added: 'The price of the passage shall be what you will.'

As magnificently Blood waved a graceful hand that was half-smothered in a foam of lace.

'That's a matter of no moment at all. Ye'll take a morning whet with us?'

'With all my heart, Captain . . .'

He paused there, waiting for the name to be supplied to him; but Captain Blood did not appear to heed. He was giving orders to the steward.

Rum and limes and sugar were brought, and over their punch they were reasonably merry, saving Hagthorpe, who was fathoms deep in preoccupation. But no sooner had Mr. Court departed than he roused himself to thank Blood for what he supposed had been in his mind when he so readily consented to carry this passenger.

'Didn't I say, now, that if you'ld put your faith in Chance, she'ld be serving us sooner or later? It's not myself ye should be thanking, Nat. It's Fortune. She's just tumbled Mr. Court out of her cornucopia into your lap.' He laughed as he mimicked Mr. Court: 'The price of the passage shall be what you will. What *you* will, Nat; and I'm thinking it's Sir James Court we'll be asking to pay it.'

3

At the very moment that Mr. Geoffrey Court was drinking that morning whet in the cabin of the *Arabella*, his cousin Sir James, a tall, spare man of fifty, as vigorous still of body as he was irresolute of mind, sat at his breakfast-table with a satchel of letters that had just arrived from England. They were letters long overdue, for the ship that had brought them, delayed and driven out of her course by gales, had exceeded by fully two months the normal time of the voyage.

Sir James had emptied the satchel onto the table, and had spread the contents for a general preliminary glance. A package bulkier than the rest drew his attention, and he took it up. He scanned the superscription with a frown that gradually drew together his heavy grizzled brows. He hesitated, passing a brown bony hand along his chin; then, as if abruptly taking a decision, he broke the seals and tore away the wrapper. From this husk he extracted a dainty volume bound in vellum, with some gold tooling on the spine and the legend, also in gold, 'The Poems of Sir John Suckling.' He sniffed contemp-

tuously, and contemptuously tossed the thing aside. But
as it fell, the volume partly opened, and at what he saw
his narrow face grew attentive. He took it up again.
The fold of vellum on the inner side of the cover had
become detached and had slightly curled away from the
board. The paste securing that fold had perished, and
as he fingered the curled edge the entire flap forming
the side of the cover came loose. Between this and the
board a folded sheet was now disclosed.

That sheet was still in Sir James's hand ten minutes
later, when the room was abruptly invaded by the dainty
lady who might have been, in years, his daughter, but
was, in fact, his wife. She was scarcely of the middle
height and virginally slight of figure, clear-eyed, and of
a delicate tint unblemished by the climate of the tropics.
She was dressed for riding, her face in the shadow of a
wide hat, a whip in her hand.

'I have to speak to you,' she announced, her voice
musical, but its tone shrewish.

Sir James, sitting with his back to the door, had not
turned to see who entered. At the sound of her voice he
dropped a napkin over the volume of poems. Then, still
without turning, he spoke:

'In that case the King's business may go to the devil.'

'Must you always sneer, sir?' The shrewish note grew
sharper. 'Do you transact the King's business at the
breakfast-table?'

Always calm, even lethargic, of spirit, Sir James re-
plied.

'Not always. No. But just as often as you must be
peremptory.'

'I don't want for cause.'

She swept forward and round the table so that she
might directly face him. She stood there, very straight,
her riding-whip in her gloved hands, held across her
slim, vigorous young body. There was a petulance on
the sensual lips, an aggressive forward thrust of the little
pointed chin.

'I have been insulted,' she announced.

Grey-faced, Sir James considered her.

'To be sure,' he said at last.

'What do you mean? "To be sure"?'

'Doesn't it happen every time that you ride out?'

'And if it does, who shall wonder when yourself you set the example?'

He avoided the offered argument. Argument, at least, was something that he had learnt to refuse this winsome termagant of half his age whom he had married five years ago and who had since poisoned his life with the bad manners and ill-temper brought from her trades-man-father's home.

'Who was it today?' asked his weary voice.

'That dog Hagthorpe. I would to God I had left him rotting in Barbados.'

'Instead of bringing him to rot here. Yes? What did he say to you?'

'Say? You don't conceive he had the effrontery to speak to me?'

He smiled a little sourly. In these days of disillusion he was able to perceive that most of the trouble came from her being too consciously a lady without proper preparation for the rôle.

'But if he insulted you?'

'It was in the cursed impudent way he looked at me, with a half-smile on his insolent face.'

'A half-smile?' The bushy brows went up. 'It may have been no more than a greeting.'

'You would say that. You would take sides even with your slaves against your wife. Happen what may, I am never in the right. Oh, no. Never. A greeting?' she sniffed. 'This was no greeting. And if it was, is a low slave to greet me with smiles?'

'A half-smile, I think you said. And as for low, he may be a slave—poor devil!—but he was born a gentle-man.'

'Fine gentleman, to be sure! A damned rebel who should have been hanged.'

His deep-set eyes gravely considered her daintiness.

'Are you quite without pity?' he asked her. 'I wonder sometimes. And is there no constancy in you either? You were so taken with the lad when first we saw him in Barbados that nothing would content you until I had bought him so that you might make of him your groom and lavish favours on him only to . . .'

Her whip crashed down on the table to interrupt him.

'I'll listen to no more of this! It's cowardly always to browbeat and bully me, and put me in the wrong. But I shall know what to do another time. I'll lay my whip across that rogue's smug face. That will teach him to leer at me.'

'It will be worthy,' was the bitter comment. 'It will be brave, towards an unfortunate who must bear whatever comes lest worse should follow.'

But she was no longer listening. The stroke of her whip had scattered some of the letters heaped upon the table. Her attention was sharply diverted.

'Has a packet come from England?' Her breathing seemed to quicken as he watched her.

'I spoke, I think, of the King's business. Here you see it. At the breakfast-table.'

She was already rummaging through the heap, scanning each package in turn. 'Are there letters for me?'

It was a second or two before his suddenly compressed lips parted again to reply evasively.

'I haven't seen all of them yet.'

She continued her search, whilst he watched her from under his brows. At the end she looked at him again.

'Nothing?' she asked, on a note of surprised, aggrieved inquiry. Her brows were knit, her delicate chin seemed to grow more pointed. 'Nothing?'

'You have looked for yourself,' he said.

She turned slowly away, her lip between finger and thumb. He was grimly amused to observe that the furious grievance with which she had sought him was forgotten; that her wrath on the matter of the slave had been quenched in another preoccupation. Slowly she moved to the door, passing out of his range of sight.

Her hand upon the knob she paused. She spoke in a voice that was soft and amiable.

'You have no word from Geoffrey?'

He answered without turning.

'I have told you that I have not yet looked through all the letters.'

Still she lingered.

'I did not see his hand on any of them.'

'In that case he has not written to me.'

'Odd!' she said slowly. 'It is very odd. We should have had word by now of when to expect him.'

'I'll not pretend to anxiety for that news.'

'You'll not?' A flush slowly inflamed her face in the pause she made. Then her anger lashed him again. 'And I? You've no thought, of course, for me, chained in this hateful island, with no society but the parson and the commandant and their silly wives. Haven't I sacrificed enough for you that you should grudge me even the rare company of someone from the world who can give me news of something besides sugar and pepper and the price of blackamoors?' She waited through a silent moment. 'Why don't you answer me?' she shrilled.

He had turned pale under his tan. He swung slowly round in his chair.

'You want an answer, do you?' There was an undertone of thunder in his voice.

Evidently she didn't. For at the mere threat of it, she went abruptly out, and slammed the door. He half-rose, and she little knew in what peril she stood at that moment from the anger that flamed up in him. Emotion of any kind, however, was short-lived in this lethargic-minded man. An imprecation fluttered from him on a sigh, as he sagged back again into his chair. Again unfolding the sheet which his hand had retained during her presence in the room, he resumed his scowling study of it. Then, having sat gloomily in thought for a long while, he rose and went to lock both the letter and the vellum-bound volume in a secretary that stood between the open windows. After that, at last, he gave his attention to the other packages that awaited him.

4

Lady Court's yearnings for society from the great world, which were at the root of a good deal of the wretchedness of that household received some satisfaction on the morrow, when the *Mary of Modena* reached the island of Nevis, that vast green mountain rising from the sea, and came to cast anchor in Charlestown Bay.

Mr. Court, all a quivering eagerness to go ashore, was in the very act of ordering Jacob, the steward, to take up his portmantles, when Captain Blood sauntered into the cabin.

'That will be for tomorrow, perhaps,' said he.

'Tomorrow?' Mr. Court stared at him. 'But this is Nevis, isn't it?'

'To be sure. This is Nevis. But before we set you ashore there's the trifling matter of the price of your passage.'

'Oh! That!' Mr. Court was contemptuous. 'Didn't I say you might make it what you please?'

'You did. And, faith, I may be taking you at your word.'

Mr. Court did not like the Captain's smile. He interpreted it in his own fashion.

'If you mean to be—ah—extortionate . . .'

'Och, not extortionate at all. Most reasonable, to be sure. Sit down, sir, whilst I explain.'

'Explain? Explain what?'

'Sit down, sir.' Blood's tone and manner were compelling.

Bewildered, Mr. Court sat down.

'It's this way,' said Captain Blood, and sat down also, on the stern locker, with his back to the open window, the sunshine, the glittering sea, and the hawkers' boats that with fruit and vegetables and fowls came crowding about the ship. 'It's this way: For the moment I'll trouble you to be considering yourself, in a manner of speaking, a hostage, Mr. Court. A hostage for a very good friend of mine, who at this moment is a slave in the hands of your cousin Sir James. You've told us how highly Sir James esteems and loves you; so there's no cause for uneasiness at all. In short, sir: my friend's freedom is the price I'll be asking Sir James for your passage. That's all.'

'All?' There was fury in Mr. Court's tone, in his prominent eyes. 'This is an outrage!'

'I'll not be depriving you of the comfort of calling it that."

Mr. Court set an obvious restraint upon his feelings. 'And supposing that Sir James should refuse.'

'Och, why will you be vexing your soul by supposing anything so unlikely? The one certain thing at present is that if Sir James consents you'll be landed at once on Nevis.'

'I am asking you, sir, what will happen if he doesn't.'

Captain Blood smiled amiably.

'I'm an orderly man, and so I like to take one thing at a time. Speculation's mostly a waste of thought. We'll leave that until it happens for the excellent reason that it may never happen at all.'

Mr. Court came to his feet in exasperation.

'But this . . . this is monstrous! Od rot me, sir, you'll do me this violence at your peril.'

'I am Captain Blood,' he was answered. 'So you'll not be supposing that a little peril more or less will daunt me.'

The announcement released some fresh emotions in Mr. Court. His eyes threatened to drop from his flushed, angry face.

'You are Captain Blood! Captain Blood! That damned pirate! You may be, but, may I perish, I care nothing who you are . . .'

'Why should you now? All I'm asking of you is that

you'll step into your cabin. Of course I shall have to place a guard at the door, but there'll be no other restraints, and your comforts shall not suffer.'

'Do you suppose I'll submit to this?'

'I can put you in irons if you prefer it,' said Captain Blood suavely.

Mr. Court, having furiously considered him, decided that he would not prefer it.

Captain Blood was rowed ashore, and took his way to the Deputy-Governor's house on the water-front: a fine white house with green slatted sunblinds set back in a fair garden where azaleas flamed and all was fragrance of orange and pimento.

He found access to Sir James an easy matter. To a person of his obvious distinction, in his becoming coat of dark blue camlet, his plumed hat, and his long sword slung from a gold-embroidered baldrick, colonial doors were readily opened. He announced himself as Captain Peter, which was scarcely false, and he left it to be supposed that his rank was naval and to be understood that the ship in which he now sailed was his own property. His business in Nevis, the most important slave-market of the West Indies, he declared to be the acquisition of a lad of whom he might make a cabin-boy. He had been informed that Sir James himself did a little slave-dealing, but even if this information were not correct, he had the presumption to hope that he might deserve Sir James's assistance in his quest.

His person was so elegantly engaging, his manner, perfectly blending deference with dignity, so winning, that Sir James professed himself entirely at Captain Peter's service. Just now there were no slaves available, but at any moment a cargo of blacks from the coast of Guinea should be arriving, and if Captain Peter were not pressed for a day or two there was no doubt that his need would be supplied. Meanwhile, of course, Captain Peter would stay to dine.

And to dine Captain Peter stayed, meeting Lady

Court, whom he impressed so favourably that before dinner was over, the invitation extended by her husband had been materially enlarged by her.

Meanwhile, considering the ostensible object of Captain Peter's visit to Nevis, it was natural that the conversation should turn to slaves, and to a comparison of the service to be obtained from them with that afforded by European servants. Sir James, by opining that the white man was so superior as to render any comparison ridiculous, opened the way for the Captain's searching probe.

'And yet all the white men out here as a result of the Monmouth Rebellion are being wasted in the plantations. It is odd that no one should ever have thought of employing any of them in some other capacity.'

'They are fit for nothing else,' said her ladyship. 'You can't make ordinary servants of such mutinous material. I know, because I tried.'

'Ah! Your ladyship tried. Now that is interesting. But you'll not be telling me that the wretches you so rescued from the plantations were so indifferent to this good fortune as not to give good service?'

Sir James interposed.

'My wife's experience is more limited than her assertion might lead you to suppose. She judges from a single trial.'

She acknowledged the hostile criticism by a disdainful glance, and the Captain came gallantly to her support.

'*Ab uno omnes,* you know, Sir James. That is often true.' He turned to the lady, who met him smiling. 'What was this single trial? What manner of man was it who proved so lacking in grace?'

'One of those rebels-convict shipped to the plantations. We found him in Barbados, and I bought him to make a groom of him. But he was so little grateful, so little sensible of that betterment of his fortunes, that in the end I sent him back to work at sugar-cane.'

The Captain's grave nod approved her.

'Faith, he was rightly served. And what became of him?'

'Just that. He's repenting his bad manners on Sir James's plantation here. A surly, mutinous dog.'

Again Sir James spoke, sadly.

'The poor wretch was a gentleman once, like so many of his misguided fellow-rebels. It was a poor mercy not to have hanged them.'

On that he changed the subject, and Captain Blood, having obtained the information that he sought, was content to allow him to do so.

But whatever the matter of which they talked, the lady's rare young beauty, combined with a sweet, ingenuous charm of manner, which seemed to bring a twist to the lip of Sir James as he watched her, commanded from their visitor the attentive regard which no man of any gallantry could have withheld. She rewarded him by insisting that whilst he waited in Charlestown he should take up his quarters in their house. She would admit of no refusal. She vowed that all the favour would be of the Captain's bestowing. Too rarely did a distinguished visitor from across the ocean come to relieve the monotony of their life on Nevis.

As a further inducement, she enlarged upon the beauties of this island. She must be the Captain's guide to its scented groves, its luxuriant plantations, its crystal streams, so that he should realize what an earthly Paradise was this which her husband had so often heard her denounce a desolate Hell.

Sir James, without illusions, covering his contempt of her light arts with a mask of grave urbanity, confirmed her invitation, whereupon she announced that she would give orders at once to have a room prepared and the Captain must send aboard for what he needed.

Captain Blood accepted this hospitality in graceful terms and without reluctance. Whilst so much may not have been absolutely necessary for the accomplishment of his purpose in Nevis, yet there could be no doubt that residence in the household of Sir James Court might very materially assist him.

5

We have heard Captain Blood expressing his faith in Fortune, or Chance as he named it to Hagthorpe. Nevertheless, he did not carry his faith to the lengths of sitting still for Fortune to come seeking him. Chances, he knew, were to be created, or at least attracted, by intelligence and diligence, and betimes on the following morning he was afoot and booted, so as to lose no time in his quest. He knew, from the information gathered yesterday, in what direction it should be pursued, and soon after sunrise he was making his way to Sir James's stables to procure the necessary means.

There could be nothing odd in that a guest of early-rising habits should choose to go for a gallop before breakfast, or that for the purpose he should borrow a mount from his host. The fact that he should elect in his ride to go by way of Sir James's plantation could hardly suggest an interest in one of the slaves at work in it.

So far, then, he could depend upon himself. Beyond that—for sight and perhaps speech of the slave he sought—he put his faith again in Fortune.

At the outset it looked as if Fortune that morning were in no kindly mood. For early though the hour, Lady Court, be it because of matutinal habits, because meticulous in her duty as a hostess, or because of an unconquerable and troublesome susceptibility to such attractiveness in the male as her guest displayed, came fresh and sprightly to take him by surprise in the stables, and to call for a horse so that she might ride with him. It was vexatious, but it did not put him out of countenance. When she joyously announced that she would show him the cascades, he secretly cursed her sprightliness. Very politely he demurred on the ground that his first interest was in the plantations.

She puckered her perfect nose in mock disdain of him.

'I vow, sir, you disappoint me. I conceived you more poetical, more romantical, a man to take joy in beauty, in the wild glories of nature.'

'Why, so I am, I hope. But I'm practical as well; and also something of a student. I can admire the orderliness of man's contriving, and inform myself upon it.'

This led to argument; a very pretty and equally silly battle of words, which Captain Blood, with a definite purpose in view, found monstrous tedious. It ended in a compromise. They rode out first to the cascades, in which she could not spur the Captain into more than languid interest, and then home to breakfast by way of the sugar plantations, in which no interest could have been more disappointingly keen to her than his. For he wasted time there, and her ladyship was growing sharpset.

So that he might view at leisure every detail, he proceeded at no more than a walking pace through the broad lanes between the walls of cane that were turning golden, past gangs of slaves, of whom a few were white, who were toiling at the irrigation trenches. From time to time the Captain would try the lady's patience by drawing rein, so that he might look about him more searchingly, and once he paused by an overseer, to question him, first on the subject of the cultivation itself, then on that of the slaves employed, their numbers and quality. He was informed that the white ones were transported convicts.

'Rebel knaves, I suppose,' said the Captain. 'Some of those psalm-singers who were out with the Duke of Monmouth.'

'Nay, sir. We've only one o' they; one as came from Barbados wi' a parcel o' thieves and cozeners. That gang's down yonder, at the end of this brake.'

They rode on and came to the group, a dozen or so half-naked, unkempt men, some of them burnt so black by the sun that they looked like pale-coloured Negroes, and more than one back a criss-cross of scars from the overseer's lash. It was amongst these that Captain Blood's questing eyes alighted on the man he sought in Nevis.

My lady, who could never long sustain a rôle of amiable docility, was beginning to manifest her loss of patience at these futilities. That loss was complete when her companion now drew rein yet again, and gave a courteous good-morning to the burly overseer of these wretched toilers. Almost at once her annoyance found an outlet. A young man, conspicuous for his athletic frame and sun-bleached golden hair, stood leaning upon his hoe, staring up wide-eyed and open-mouthed at the Captain.

She urged her mare forward.

'Why do you stand idle, oaf? Will you never learn not to stare at your betters? Then here's to improve your manners.'

Viciously her riding-switch cut across his naked shoulders. It was raised again, to repeat the stroke; but the slave, who had half-swung round so as fully to face her, parried the blow on his left forearm as it descended whilst his hand, simultaneously closing upon the switch, wrenched it from her with a jerk that almost pulled her from the saddle.

If the other toilers fell idle, to stare in awe, there was instant action from the watchful overseer. With an oath he sprang for the young slave, uncoiling the thong of his whip.

'Cut the flesh from his bones, Walter!' shrilled the lady.

Before this menace the goaded youth flung away the silver-mounted switch and swung his hoe aloft. His light eyes were blazing.

'Touch me with that whip, and I'll beat your brains out.'

The big overseer checked. He knew reckless resolve when he saw it, and here it glared at him plainly. The slave, maddened by pain and injustice, was no more in case to count the cost of doing as he threatened than of having dared to employ the threat. The overseer attempted to dominate him by words and tone, so as to gain time until the frenzy should have passed.

'Put down that hoe, Hagthorpe. Put it down at once.'

But Hagthorpe laughed at him; and then my lady laughed, too, on a note that was horrible in its evil, spiteful glee.

'Don't argue with the dog. Pistol him! You've my warrant for it, Walter. I'm witness to his mutiny. Pistol him, man.'

Thus insistently and imperatively ordered, the man carried a hand to the holster at his belt. But even as he drew the weapon, the Captain leaned over from the saddle, and the butt of his heavy riding-crop crashed upon the overseer's hand, sending the pistol flying. The fellow cried out in pain and amazement.

'Be easy now,' said Blood; 'I've saved your life, so I have. For it would have cost you no less if you had fired that pistol.'

'Captain Peter!' It was a cry of indignant, incredulous protest from Lady Court.

He turned to her, and the scorn in his eyes, so vividly blue under their black brows, struck her like a blow.

'What are you? A woman? Od's blood, ma'am, in London Town I've seen poor street-walkers carted that were more womanly.'

She gasped. Then fury rallied her courage to answer him.

'I have a husband, sir, I thank God. You shall answer to him for that.' She drove a vicious spur into her horse, and departed at the gallop, leaving him to follow as he listed.

'Sure and I'll answer to all the husbands in the world,' he called after her, and laughed.

Then he beckoned Hagthorpe forward.

'Here, my lad. You'll come and answer with me. I am going to see justice done, and I know better than to leave you at the mercy of an overseer while I'm about it. Take hold of my stirrup-leather. You're coming with me to Sir James. Stand back there, my man, or I'll ride you down. It's to your master I'll be accounting for my actions; not to you.'

Still nursing his hand, the overseer, his face sullen, fell aside before that threat, and Captain Blood moved on at an easy pace down the golden lane with Tom Hagthorpe striding beside him clinging to his stirrup-leather. Out of earshot the young man hoarsely asked a question.

'Peter, by what miracle do you happen here?'

'Miracle, is it? Now didn't ye suppose that sooner or later one or another of us would be coming to look for you?' He laughed. 'I've not only had the luck to find you. That sweet, womanly creature has supplied a pretext for my interest in you. It makes things easy. And, anyway, easy or difficult, by my soul, I'm not leaving Nevis without you.'

6

In the hall of the Deputy-Governor's house, when they came to it, Captain Blood left the lad to wait for him, whilst guided by my lady's strident, scolding voice he strode to the dining-room. There he found Sir James seated, cold and sneering, before a neglected breakfast and her ladyship pacing the room as she railed. The opening of the door momentarily checked her. Then, with heaving breast and eyes that flamed in a white face, she exploded at the intruder.

'You have the effrontery to present yourself!'

'I thought that I might be expected.'

'Expected? Ha!'

He bowed a little.

'I'm far from wishing to intrude. But I suppose that some explanation might be desired of me.'

'Some explanation, indeed!'

'And it's not in my sensitive heart to disappoint a lady.'

'Awhile ago you had another name for me.'

'Awhile ago you deserved another.'

Sir James rapped the table. His dignity both as Deputy-Governor and as husband demanded, he conceived, this intervention.

'Sir!' His tone was a reproof. Peremptorily he added: 'A plain tale if you please.'

'Faith, I'll make it plainer than may please you, Sir James. I'll not be mincing words at all.' And forth came a scrupulous account of the events, in the course of rendering which he was more than once compelled to overbear her ladyship's interruptions.

At the end her husband looked at her where she stood fuming, and there was no sympathy in his glance. It was cold and hard and laden with dislike.

'Captain Peter supplies what the tale lacked to make it hang together.'

'It should suffice, at least, to show you that satisfaction is required, unless you're a poltroon.'

Whilst the Deputy-Governor was wincing at the insult, Captain Blood was making haste to interpose.

'Sir James, I am at your service for satisfaction of whatever sort you choose. But first, for my own satisfaction, let me say that, if under the spur of emotions which I trust you will account humane, I have done aught that is offensive, my apologies are freely offered.'

Sir James remained singularly cold and stern.

'You have done little good, and perhaps a deal of harm, by your intervention. This wretched slave, encouraged to mutiny by your action, cannot be suffered to escape the consequences. There would be an end to order and discipline in the plantation if his conduct were overlooked. You perceive that?'

'Does it matter what he perceives?' railed the lady.

'What I perceive is that if I had not intervened this man would have been shot on the spot by her ladyship's orders, and this, because innocent of all offence, he resisted the threat—again by her ladyship's orders—of having the flesh cut from his bones. Those were her gentle words.'

'It is certainly what will happen to him now,' she spitefully announced. 'That is, unless Sir James prefers to hang him.'

'As a scapegoat for me, because I intervened?' demanded the Captain of Sir James, and Sir James, stung by the sneer, made haste to answer:

'No, no. For threatening the overseer.'

This brought down upon him a fresh attack from her ladyship.

'His insolence to me, of course, is of no account. Nor, it seems, is this gentleman's.'

Between the two of them, Sir James was in danger of losing his stern habitual calm. He slapped the table so that the dishes rattled.

'One thing at a time, madam, if you please. The situation is nasty enough, God knows. I've warned you more than once against venting your spleen upon this fellow Hagthorpe. Now you force me to choose between flogging him for an insubordination that I cannot regard as other than fully provoked, and imperilling all discipline among the slaves. Since I cannot afford that, I have to thank your tantrums, madam, for compelling me to be inhuman.'

'Whilst I have none but myself to thank for having mated with a fool!'

'That, madam, is a matter we may presently have occasion to argue,' said he, and there was something so mysteriously minatory in his tone that sheer astonishment deprived her pertness of an answer.

Softly Blood's voice cut into the pause.

'I might be able, Sir James, to lift you from the horns of this dilemma.' And he went on to explain himself. 'You'll remember that it was to buy a cabin-boy I landed here. I had thought of a Negro; but this Hagthorpe seems a likely lad. Sell him to me, and I'll take him off your hands.'

The elderly man considered a moment, and his gloom was seen to lighten a little.

'Egad! It's a solution.'

'You have but to name your price, then, Sir James.'

But her ladyship was there with her spite to close that easy exit.

'What next? The man's a rebel-convict, doomed for life to service in the plantations. You have a clear duty. You dare not be a party to his leaving the West Indies.'

In the troubled hesitation of that irresolute man, Blood saw that all was not yet done, as he had hoped. Cursing the spite of the lovely termagant, he advanced to the foot of the table, and, folding his arms on the tall back of the chair that stood there, he looked grimly from one to other of them.

'Well, well!' said he. 'And so this unfortunate lad is to be flogged.'

'He's to be hanged,' her ladyship corrected.

'No, no,' Sir James protested. 'A flogging will suffice.'

'I see that I can do no more,' said Blood, and his manner became ironically smooth. 'So I'll take my leave. But before I go, Sir James, there's something I'd almost forgot. I found a cousin of yours at Saint Thomas who was in haste to get to Nevis.'

He intended to surprise them; and he succeeded; but their surprise was no greater than his own at the abrupt and utter change of manner his announcement produced in her ladyship.

'Geoffrey!' she cried, a catch in her voice. 'Do you mean Geoffrey Court?'

'That is his name. Geoffrey Court.'

'And he's at Saint Thomas, you say?' Again it was her ladyship who questioned him, the change in her manner growing more ludicrously marked. There was a change too in the aspect of Sir James. He was observing his wife from under his bushy eyebrows, the ghost of a sneer on his thin lips.

'No, no,' Blood corrected. 'Mr. Court is here. Aboard my ship. I gave him passage from Saint Thomas.'

'Then . . .' she paused. She was out of breath, and her brows were knit in a puzzled frown. 'Then why has he not landed?'

'I'm disposed to think it's by a dispensation of Providence. Just as it was by a dispensation of Providence that he requested a passage of me. All that need matter to you, Sir James, is that he's still aboard.'

'But is he ill, then?' cried my lady.

'As healthy as a fish, ma'am. But he may not so continue. Aboard that ship, Sir James, I am as absolute as you are here ashore.'

It was impossible to misunderstand him. Taken aback, they stared at him a moment, then her ladyship, panting and quavering, exploded.

'There are laws to restrain you, I suppose.'

'No laws at all, ma'am. You have only half my name. I am Captain Peter, yes. Captain Peter Blood.' It had become necessary to disclose himself if his threat was to carry weight. He smiled upon their silent stupefaction. 'Perhaps you'll be seeing the need, for the sake of Cousin Geoffrey, of being more humane in the matter of this unfortunate slave. For I give you my word that whatever you do to young Hagthorpe, that same will I do to Mr. Geoffrey Court.'

Sir James actually and incomprehensibly laughed, whilst her ladyship gaped in terror for a moment before bracing herself to deal practically with the situation.

'Before you can do anything you'll have to reach your ship again, and you'll never leave Charlestown until Mr. Court is safely ashore. You've forgotten to . . .'

'Och, I've forgotten nothing,' he interrupted, with a wave of the hand. 'You're not to suppose that I'm the man to walk into a gin without taking precautions to see that it can't be sprung on me. The *Mary of Modena* carries forty guns in her flanks, all of them demi-cannons. Two of her broadsides will make of Charlestown just a heap of rubble. And it's what'll happen if they have no word of me aboard before eight bells is made. You'll come away from that bell-pull, my lady, if you're prudent.'

She came away, white and trembling, whilst Sir

James, grey-faced, but still with that suggestion of a sneering smile about his lips, looked up at Captain Blood.

'You play the highwayman, sir. You put a pistol to our heads.'

'No pistol at all. Just forty demi-cannons, and every one of them loaded.'

But for all his bravado, Captain Blood fully realized that in the pass to which things were come he might yet have to pistol Sir James so as to win free. He would deplore the necessity; but he was prepared for it. What he was not prepared for was the Deputy-Governor's abrupt and easy acquiescence.

'That simplifies the issue, which is, I think, that whatever I do to Hagthorpe, you will do to my cousin.'

'That is the issue exactly.'

'Then, if I were to hang Hagthorpe.'

'There would be a yardarm for your cousin.'

'Only one decision, of course, is possible.'

Her ladyship's gasp of relief from her mounting fears was clearly audible.

'You prevail, sir,' she cried. 'We must let Hagthorpe go.'

'On the contrary,' said Sir James, 'I must hang him.'

'You must . . .' She choked as she stared at him, open-mouthed, the horror back again in her wide blue eyes.

'I have a clear duty, madam, as you reminded me. As you said, I dare not be a party to Hagthorpe's leaving the plantations. He must hang. *Fiat justitia, ruat coelum.* I think that's how it runs. What happens afterwards will not be on my conscience.'

'Not on your conscience!' She was distraught. 'But Geoffrey!' She wrung her hands. 'Geoffrey!' Her tone had become a wail. Then, rallying, she turned in fury on her husband. 'You're mad! Mad! You can't do this! You can't! Hagthorpe must go. What does he matter, after all? What's a slave more or less? In God's name, let him go.'

'And my duty, then? My clear duty?'

His sternness broke her spirit. 'Oh, God!' She flung herself on her knees beside his chair clawing his arm in her anguish.

He cast her off and answered her with a laugh that in its contemptuous mockery was horrible to hear.

Afterwards Captain Blood boasted, perhaps unduly, that it was this cruel amusement at the woman's panic that brought light to a situation full of mystery, explained the ready acceptance of it by Sir James, and made plain much else that had been puzzling.

Having laughed his wicked fill, the Deputy-Governor rose, and waved a hand in dismissal of the Captain.

'The matter's settled, then. You'll desire to return to your ship, and I'll not detain you. Yet, stay. You might take a message to my cousin.' He went to unlock the secretary that stood between the windows. Thence he took a copy of 'The Poems of Sir John Suckling,' on one of the sides of which the vellum curled away from the board. 'Condole with him on my behalf, and restore him this. I was waiting for him, to hand it to him, myself. But it will be much better this way. Assure him from me that the letter it contained, almost as poetical as the volume itself, has now been faithfully delivered.' And to her ladyship he held out a folded sheet. 'It is for you, ma'am. Take it.' She shrank in fear. 'Take it,' he insisted, and flung it at her. 'We will discuss its contents presently. Meanwhile, it will help you to understand my strict regard for that clear duty of which you reminded me.'

Crouching where he had left her beside his empty chair, her shaking fingers unfolded the sheet. She lowered her eyes to the writing; then, after a moment, with a whimpering sound, let the sheet fall.

Captain Blood was taking in his hands the volume that Sir James had proffered. It was now, I think, that full understanding came to him, and for a moment he was in a dilemma. If the unexpected had helped him at the commencement, the unexpected had certainly come to thwart him now, when in sight of the end.

'I'll wish you a very good day, sir,' said Sir James. 'There is nothing to detain you longer.'

'You're in a mistake, Sir James. There's just one thing. I've changed my mind. I may have done many things in my time for which I should take shame. But I've never yet been anyone's hangman, and I'll be damned if I fill that office in your service. I was quite ready to hang this cousin of yours as an act of reprisal. But I'm damned if I'll hang him to oblige you. I'll send him ashore, Sir James, so that you may hang him yourself.'

The sudden dismay in Sir James's face was no more than Captain Blood expected. Having thus wrecked that sweet plan of vengeance, the Captain went on to show where consolation lay.

'If now that I've changed my mind, you were to change yours, and sell me this lad to be my cabin-boy, I'd not only carry your cousin away with me, but I think I could induce him not to trouble you again.'

Sir James's deep-set eyes questioningly searched the face of the buccaneer.

Captain Blood smiled. 'It's entirely a friendly proposal, Sir James,' he said, and the assurance bore conviction to the troubled mind of the Deputy-Governor.

'Very well,' he said at last. 'You may take the lad. On those terms I make you a gift of him.'

7

Realizing that husband and wife would be having a good deal to say to each other, and that to linger at such a time would be intrusive, Captain Blood took an immediate, tactful leave, and departed.

In the hall he summoned the waiting Tom Hagthorpe to accompany him, and the lad, understanding nothing of this amazing deliverance, went with him.

None hindering them, they hired a boat at the mole,

and so came to the *Mary of Modena,* in the waist of
which the two brothers, reunited, fell into each other's
arms, whilst Captain Blood looked on with all the sense
of being a beneficent deity.

On the verge of tears, Nat demanded to know by
what arts Peter Blood had accomplished this deliverance
so speedily and without violence.

'I'll not be saying there was no violence,' said Blood.
'There was, in fact, a deal of it. But it was violence of
the emotions. And there's some more of the same kind
to be borne yet. But that's for Mr. Court.' He turned to
the bos'n who was standing by. 'Pipe the hands to quarters, Jake. We weigh at once.'

He went off to the cabin to which Mr. Court was confined. He dismissed the guard posted at the door, and
unlocked it. A very furious gentleman greeted him.

'How much longer do you keep me here, you damned
scoundrel?'

'And where would you be going, now?' wondered
Captain Blood.

'Where would I be going? D'ye mock me, you cursed
pirate? I'm going ashore, as you well know.'

'Do I, now? I wonder.'

'D'ye mean still to prevent me?'

'Faith, there may not be the need. I have a message
for you from Sir James: a message and a book of
poetry.'

Faithfully he delivered both. Mr. Court changed colour, went limp, and sat down suddenly on a locker.

'Perhaps you'll be less eager now to land on Nevis. It
may begin to occur to you that the West Indies are not
the healthiest region for dalliance. Jealousy in the tropics can be like the climate; mighty hot and fierce. You'll
wisely prefer, I should think, to find a ship somewhere
that will carry you safely home to England.'

Mr. Court wiped the perspiration from his brow.

'Then you're not putting me ashore?'

The thudding of the capstan and the rattle of the
anchor-chain reached them through the open port of the

cabin. Captain Blood's gesture drew attention to the sound.

'We are weighing now. We shall be at sea in half-an-hour.'

'Perhaps it's as well,' Mr. Court resignedly admitted.

Sacrilege

1

NEVER IN THE whole course of his outlawry did Captain Blood cease to regard it as distressingly ironical that he who was born and bred in the Romish Faith should owe his exile from England to a charge of having supported the Protestant Champion and should be regarded by Spain as a heretic who would be the better for a burning.

He expatiated at length and aggrievedly upon this to Yberville, his French associate, on a day when he was constrained by inherent scruples to turn his back upon a prospect of great and easy plunder to be made at the cost of a little sacrilege.

Yet Yberville, whose parents had hoped to make a churchman of him, and who had actually been in minor orders before circumstances sent him overseas and turned him into a filibuster instead, was left between indignation and amusement at scruples which he accounted vain. Amusement, however, won the day with him; for this tall and vigorous fellow, already inclining a little to portliness, was of as jovial and easy-going a nature as his humorous mouth and merry brown eye announced. Undoubtedly—although in the end he was to provoke derision by protesting it—a great churchman had been lost in him.

They had put into Bieque, and ostensibly for the purpose of buying stores, Yberville had gone ashore to see what news might be gleaned that could be turned to account. For this was at a time when the *Arabella* was sailing at a venture, without definite object. A Basque who had spent some years across the border in Spain, Yberville spoke a fluent Castilian which enabled him to pass for a Spaniard when he chose, and so equipped him perfectly for this scouting task in a Spanish settlement.

He had come back to the big red-hulled ship at anchor in the roadstead, with the flag of Spain impudently flaunted from her maintruck, with news that seemed to him to indicate a likely enterprise. He had learnt that Don Ignacio de la Fuente, sometime Grand Inquisitor of Castile, and now appointed Cardinal-Archbishop of New Spain, was on his way to Mexico on the eighty-gun galleon, the *Santa Veronica,* and in passing was visiting the bishoprics of his province. His eminence had been at San Salvador, and he was now reported on his way to San Juan de Puerto Rico, after which he was expected at San Domingo, perhaps at Santiago de Cuba, and certainly at Havana, before finally crossing to the Main.

Unblushingly Yberville disclosed the profit which his rascally mind conceived might be extracted from these circumstances.

'Next to King Philip himself,' he opined, 'or, at least, next to the Grand Inquisitor, the Cardinal-Archbishop of Seville, there is no Spaniard living who would command a higher ransom than this Primate of New Spain.'

Blood checked in his stride. The two were pacing the high poop of the *Arabella* in the bright November sunshine of that region of perpetual summer. Yberville's tall vigour was still set off by the finery of lilac satin in which he had gone ashore, a purple love-knot in his long brown curls. Forward at the capstan and at the braces was the bustle of preparation to get the great ship under way; and in the forechains, Snell, the bos'n, his bald pate gleaming in a circlet of untidy grey curls, was ordering in obscene Castilian some bumboats to stand off.

Blood's vivid eyes flashed disapproval upon the jovial countenance of his companion.

'What, then?' he asked.

'Why, just that. The *Santa Veronica* carries a sacerdotal cargo as rich as the plate in any ship that ever came out of Mexico.' And he laughed.

But Blood did not laugh with him.

'I see. And it's your blackguardly notion that we should lay her board and board, and seize the Archbishop?'

'Just that, my faith! The place to lie in wait for the *Santa Veronica* would be the straits north of Saona. There we should catch his eminence on his way to San Domingo. It should offer little difficulty.'

Under the shade of his broad hat Blood's countenance had become forbidding. He shook his head.

'That is not for us.'

'Not for us? Why not? Are you deterred by her eighty guns?'

'I am deterred by nothing but the trifle of sacrilege concerned. To lay violent hands on an archbishop, and hold him to ransom! I may be a sinner, God knows; but underneath it all, I hope I'm a true son of the Church.'

'You mean a son of the true Church,' Yberville amended. 'I hope I'm no less myself, but not on that account would I make a scruple of holding a Grand Inquisitor to ransom.'

'Maybe not. But then you had the advantage of being bred in a seminary. That makes you free, I suppose, with holy things.'

Yberville laughed at the sarcasm.

'It makes me discriminate between the Faith of Rome and the Faith of Spain. Your Spaniard, with his Holy House, his *autos-da-fé,* and his faggots, is very nearly a heretic in my eyes.'

'A sophistry, to justify the abduction of a cardinal. But I'm not a sophist, Yberville, whatever else I may be. We'll keep out of sacrilege, so we will.'

Before the determination in his tone and face, Yberville fetched a sigh of resignation.

'Well, well! If that's your feeling . . . But it's a great chance neglected.'

And it was now that Captain Blood dilated upon the

irony of his fate, until from the capstan to interrupt him came the bos'n's cry: 'Belay there!' Then his whistle shrilled, and men swarmed aloft to let go the clew lines. The *Arabella* shook out her sails as a bird spreads its wings, and stood out for the open sea, to continue at a venture, without definite aim.

In leisurely fashion, with the light airs prevailing, they skimmed about the Virgin Islands, keeping a sharp lookout for what might blow into their range; but not until some three or four days later, when perhaps a score of miles to the south of Puerto Rico, did they sight a likely quarry. This was a small two-masted carack, very high in the poop, carrying not more than a dozen guns, and obviously a Spaniard, from the picture of Our Lady of Sorrows on the ballooning mainsail.

The *Arabella* shifted a point or two nearer to the wind, hoisted the Union flag, and coming within range put a shot across the Spaniard's bows, as a signal to heave-to.

Considering the presumed Englishman's heavy armament and superior sailing power, it is not surprising that the carack should have been prompt to obey that summons. But it was certainly a surprising contradiction to the decoration of her mainsail that simultaneously with her coming up into the wind, the Cross of Saint George should break from her maintruck. After that she lowered a boat, and sent it speeding across the quarter-mile of gently ruffled sapphire water to the *Arabella*.

Out of this boat, a short, stockily built man, red of hair and of face, decently dressed in bottle green, climbed the Jacob's-ladder of Blood's ship. With purposefulness in every line of him, he rolled forward on short, powerful legs towards Captain Blood, who in a stateliness of black-and-silver, waited to receive him in the ship's waist. Blood was supported there by the scarcely less splendid Yberville, the giant Wolverstone, who had left an eye at Sedgemoor and boasted that with the one remaining he could see twice as much as any ordinary man, and Jeremy Pitt, the sailing master of the

Arabella, from whose entertaining chronicles we derive this account of the affair.

Pitt sums up this newcomer in a sentence. 'Not in all my life did I ever see a hotter man.' There was a scorching penetration in the glance of his small eyes under their beetling sandy brows as they raked his surroundings: the deck that was clean-scoured as a trencher, the gleaming brass of the scuttle-butts and of the swivel-gun on the poop-rail, the orderly array of muskets in the rack about the mainmast. All may well have led him to suppose that he was aboard a King's ship.

Finally his questing hazel eyes returned to a second and closer inspection of the waiting group.

'My name is Walker,' he announced, with a truculent air and in an accent that proclaimed a northern origin. 'Captain Walker. And I'll be glad to know who the devil you may be that ye're so poxy ready with your gunfire. If ye've put a shot athwart my bows, 'cause o' they emblems o' popery on my mains'l, supposing me a Spaniard, faith, then, ye're just the men I be looking for.'

Blood was austere.

'If you are the captain of that ship, it's glad I'd be to learn how that comes to be the case.'

'Ay, ay. So ye may, ecod! It's a long tale, Cap'n, and an ugly.'

Blood took the hint.

'Come below,' he said, 'and let us have it.'

It was in the great cabin of the *Arabella,* with its carved and gilded bulkheads, its hangings of green damask, its costly plate and books and pictures and other sybaritic equipment such as the rough little North Country seaman had never dreamed could be found under a ship's deck, that the tale was told. It was told to the four who had received this odd visitor, and after Blood had presented himself and his associates, thereby momentarily abating some of the little shipmaster's truculence. But he recovered all his heat and fury when they came to sit about the table, on which the Negro steward had set Canary sack and Nantes brandy and a

jug of bumbo, brewed of rum and sugar, water and nut-
meg, and it roared in him as he related what he had en-
dured.

He had sailed, he told them, from Plymouth, six
months earlier, bound in the first instance for the coast
of Guinea, where he had taken aboard three hundred
able-bodied young Negroes, bought with beads and
knives and axes from an African chieftain with whom
he had already previously done several similar tradings.
With this valuable cargo under hatches he was making
his way to Jamaica, where a ready market awaited him,
when, at the end of September, somewhere off the
Bahamas, he was caught by an early storm, forerunner
of the approaching hurricane season.

'By the mercy o' God we came through it afloat. But
we was so battered and feckless that I had to jettison all
my guns. Under the strain we had sprung a leak that
kept us pumping for our lives; most o' my upper works
was gone, and my mizzen was in such a state that I
couldna wi' safety ha' spread a night-shift on it. I must
run to the nearest port for graving, and the nearest port
happened to be Havana.

'When the Port Alcalde had come aboard, seen for
hisself my draggle-tailed condition, and that, anyway,
wi'out guns I were toothless, as ye might say, he let me
come into the shelter o' the lagoon, and there, without
careening, we set about repairs.

'To pay for what we lacked I offered to trade the
Alcalde some o' they blacks I carried. Now happen, as
I was to learn, that the mines had been swept by a
plague o' some kind—smallpox or yellow fever or sum-
mut—and they was mighty short o' slaves to work them.
The Alcalde would buy the lot, he says, if I would sell.
Seeing how it was with me, I were glad enough to
lighten the ship by being rid o' the whole cargo, and I
looked on the Alcalde's need as a crowning mercy to get
me out of all my difficulties. But that weren't the end o'
the windfall, as I supposed it. Instead o' gold, the
Alcalde proposed to me that I takes payment in green
hides, which, as ye may know, is the chief product of the

island of Cuba. Naught could ha' suited me better, for I knew as I could sell the hides in England for three times the purchase price, and maybe a trifle over. So he gives me a bill o' lading for the hides, which it were agreed we should take aboard so soon as we was fit to sail.

'I pushed on wi' repairs, counting my fortune made, and looking on a voyage that at one time had seemed as if it must end in shipwreck, like to prove the most profitable as I had ever made.

'But I were reckoning without Spanish villainy. For when we was at last in case to put to sea again, and I sends word to the Alcalde that we was ready to load the hides of his bill o' lading, the mate, which I had sent ashore, comes me back wi' a poxy message that the Captain-General—as they call the Governor in Cuba— would not allow the shipment, seeing as how it was against the law for any foreigner to trade in a Spanish settlement, and the Alcalde advised us to put to sea at once, whilst the Captain-General was in a mind to permit it.

'Ye'll maybe guess my feelings. Tom Walker, I may tell ye, bain't the man to let hisself be impudently robbed by anyone, whether pickpocket or Captain-General. So I goes ashore myself. Not to the Alcalde. Oh, no. I goes straight to the Captain-General hisself, a high-and-mighty Castilian grande, wi' a name as long as my arm. For short, they calls him Don Ruiz Perera de Valdoro y Peñascon, no less, and he's Count of Marcos, too. A grande of the grandest.

'I slaps down my bill o' lading afore him, and tells him straightly how the thieving Alcalde had dealt by me, certain sure in my fecklessness that justice would be done at once.

'But from the way he shrugged and smiled, I knew him for a villain afore ever he spoke. "Ye've been told the law, I believe," says he, wi' a fleering curl to his mangy lip. "And ye've been rightly told. It is forbidden us by decree of His Catholic Majesty to buy from or sell to any foreign trader. The hides may not be shipped."

'It were a sour disappointment to me, seeing the

profit on which I'd reckoned. But I keeps my temper to myself. "So be it," says I, "although it comes mighty hard on me, and the law might ha' been thought of afore I were given this poxy bill o' lading. Howsomever, here it be; and ye can have it back in return for my three hundred Negroes."

'At that he scowls and tries to stare me down, twirling his moustaches the while. "God gi' me patience wi' you!" says he. "That transaction, too, were illegal. Ye had no right to trade your slaves here."

' "I traded them at the Alcalde's request, excellency," I reminds him.

' "My friend," says he, "if you was to commit murder at someone else's request, would that excuse the crime?"

' "It's not me who's broken the law," says I, "but him which bought the slaves from me."

' "Ye're both guilty. Therefore, neither must profit. The slaves is confiscated to the State."

'Now I've told ye, sirs, as how I was making no ado about suffering the loss of my lawful profit on the hides. But to be stripped naked, as it were, by that heuck-fingered Spanish gentleman, robbed o' a cargo o' blacks, the worth o' which I had agreed at ten thousand pieces of eight—Od rot my soul!—that was more nor I could stomach. My temper got the better o' me, and I ups and storms in a mighty rage at that fine Castilian nobleman —Don Ruiz Perera de Valdoro y Peñascon—crying shame on him for such iniquity, and demanding that at least he pay me in gold the price o' my slaves.

'The cool villain lets me rant myself out, then shows me his teeth again in another o' his wicked, fleering smiles.

' "My friend," says he, "ye've no cause to make this pother, no cause to complain at all. Why, you heretic fool, let me tell you as I am doing far less than my strict duty, which would be to seize your ship, your crew, and your person, and send you to Cadiz or Seville, there to purge the heresies wi' which your kind be troubling the world." '

Captain Walker paused there, to compose himself a little from the passion into which his memories had whipped him. He mopped his brow, and took a pull at the bumbo before resuming.

'Od rot me for a coward, but my courage went out o' me like sweat at they words. Better be robbed, says I to myself, than be cast into the Fires o' the Faith in a fool's coat. So I takes my leave of his excellency afore his sense o' duty might get the better o' what he calls his compassion— damn his dirty soul!'

Again he paused, and then went on. 'Ye may be supposing that the end o' my trouble. But bide awhile; for it weren't, nor yet the worst.

'I gets back aboard in haste, as ye'll understand. We weighs at once, and slips out to sea without no interference from the forts. But we've not gone above four or five miles to sea, when on our heels comes a carack of a *guarda-costa,* and opens fire on us as soon as ever she's within range. It's my belief she had orders from the mucketty Captain-General to sink us. And for why? Because his talk of the Holy Office and the fires of the Faith was so much bluster. The last thing as that thief would wish would be as they should find out in Spain the ways by which he is becoming rich in the New World.

'Howsomever, there was the *guarda-costa,* pumping round shot into us as fast and hard as bad Spanish gunnery could contrive it. Without guns as we was, it were easy as shooting woodcock. Or so they thought. But, having the weather-gauge o' them, I took the only chance left us. I put the helm hard over, and ran straight for her. Not a doubt but those muck-scutcheons counted on shooting us to pieces afore ever we could reach her, and, on my soul, they all but did. We was sinking fast, leaking like a colander, wi' our decks awash when at last we bumps alongside o' her. But by the mercy o' God to heretics, what were left o' my poor ship got a hold on that *guarda-costa's* timbers wi' her grapnels, what time we climbed aboard her. After that it were red

hell on they decks, for we was all mad wi' rage at those
cold-blooded murderers. From stem to stern we swept
her wi' cold steel. I had five men killed and a half-score
wounded; but the only Spaniards left alive was them as
went overboard to drown.'

The slaver paused again, and his fiery eye flung a
glance of challenge at his audience.

'That's about all, I think. We kept the carack, of
course, my own ship being sunk, and that'll explain they
emblems o' Popery on our mainsail. I knew as they'ld
bring us trouble afore long. And yet, when, as I supposed, it was on account o' they that ye put a shot
athwart my hawse, it came to me that maybe I had
found a friend.'

2

The tale was told, and the audience, thrilled and
moved by it, sat in silence awhile, still under the spell
of it after Walker had ceased to speak.

It was Wolverstone, at last, who stirred and growled.

'As ugly a story as I've heard of Castilian subtlety.
That Captain-General would be the better for a keel-
hauling.'

'Better still for a roasting over a slow fire,' said Yberville. 'It's the only way to give savour to this New
Christian pig.'

Blood looked at him across the table.

'New Christian?' he echoed. 'You know him, then?'

'No more than you.' And the sometime seminarist explained. 'In Spain when a Jew is received into the
Church he must take a new name. But his choice is not
entirely free. The name he takes must be the name of a
tree or plant, or the like, so that the source of his house
may still be known. This Captain-General bears the
name of Perera: Pear-tree. The Valdoro and Peñascon
have been subsequently added. They are always the
readiest, these renegadoes, with threats of the fires of the
Faith.'

Blood gave his attention once more to Captain Walker.

'You'll have a purpose, sir, in giving yourself the trouble of telling us this nasty tale. What service do you seek of us?'

'Why, just a spare set o' sails, if so be ye have them, as I'm supposing ye will. I'll pay you what they're worth; for, burn me, it's inviting trouble to try to cross the ocean with those I carry.'

'And is that all, now! Faith, it was in my mind ye might be asking us to recover the value of your slaves from this Captain-General of Havana, with perhaps just a trifle over for our trouble in the interests of poetic justice. Havana is a wealthy city.'

Walker stared at him.

'Ye're laughing at me, Captain. I know better than to ask the impossible.'

'The impossible!' said Blood, with a lift of his black brows. Then he laughed. 'On my soul, it's almost like a challenge.'

'No challenge at all. Ye'll be bonny fighters, like enough; but the Devil himself wouldn't venture to sail a buccaneer ship into Havana.'

'Ah!' Blood rubbed his chin. 'Yet this fellow needs a lesson, bad cess to him. And to rob a thief is a beckoning adventure.' He looked at his associates. 'Will we be paying him a visit, now?'

Pitt's opposition was immediate.

'Not unless we've taken leave of our senses. You don't know Havana, Peter. If there's a Spanish harbour in the New World that may be called impregnable, that harbour is Havana. In all the Caribbean there are no defences more formidable, as Drake discovered already in his day.'

'And that's the fact,' said Walker, whose red eye had momentarily gleamed at Blood's words. 'The place is an arsenal. The entrance is by a channel not more than half a mile across, with three forts, no less, to defend it: the

Moro, the Puntal, and El Fuerte. Ye wouldn't stay afloat an hour there.'

Blood's eyes were dreamy. 'Yet you stayed afloat some days.'

'Ay, man. But the circumstances.'

'Glory be, now. Couldn't we be contriving circumstances? It wouldn't be the first time. The thing needs thought, and it's worth thinking about with no other enterprise to engage us.'

'That,' said Yberville, who could not reconcile himself quite to the neglect of the opportunity presented by the voyage of the Archbishop, 'is only because you're mawkish. The Primate of the New World is still at sea. Let him pay for the sins of his countrymen. His ransom need be no less than the plunder of Havana would yield us, and we could include in it compensation for Captain Walker for the slaves of which they've robbed him.'

'Faith, ye have it,' said Wolverstone, who, being a heretic, was undaunted by any thought of sacrilege. 'It's like burning candles to Satan to be delicate with a Spaniard just because he's an archbishop.'

'And it need not end there,' said Pitt, that other heretic, in a glow of sudden inspiration. 'If we had the Archbishop in the hold, we could sail into Havana without fear of their forts. They'd never dare to fire on a ship that housed his holiness.'

Blood was pensively toying with a curl of his black periwig. He smiled introspectively.

'I was thinking that same.'

'So!' crowed Yberville. 'Religious scruples begin to yield to reason. Heaven be praised.'

'Faith, now, I'll not say that it might not be worth a trifle of sacrilege—just a trifle, mark you—to squeeze his plunder out of this rogue of a Captain-General. Yes, I think it might be done.' He got up suddenly. 'Captain Walker, if ye've a mind to come with us on this venture and seek to recover what ye've lost, ye'd best be scuttling that *guarda-costa* and fetching your hands aboard the *Arabella*. Ye can trust us to provide you with a ship to take you home when this is over.'

'Man!' cried the tough little slaver, all the natural fierceness of him sunk fathoms deep in his amazement. 'Ye're not serious?'

'Not very,' said Captain Blood. 'It's just a whim of mine. But a whim that is like to cost this Don What's-his-name Perera dear. So you can come with us to Havana, and take your chance of sailing home again in a tall ship with a full cargo of hides, your fortunes restored, or you can have the set of sails ye're asking for, and go home empty-handed. The choice is yours.'

Looking up at him almost in awe, Captain Walker yielded at once to the vigorous vitality and full-blooded confidence of the buccaneer. The adventurous spirit in him answered to the call. No risk, he swore, was too great that offered a chance to wipe off the score against that forsworn Captain-General.

Yberville, however, was frowning.

'But the Archbishop, then?'

Blood smiled with tight lips.

'The Archbishop certainly. We can do nothing without the Archbishop.' He turned to Pitt with an order that showed how fully he had already resolved not only upon what was to do, but upon how it should be done. 'Jerry, you'll lay me a course for Sainte-Croix.'

'Why that?' quoth Yberville. 'It's much farther east than we need to go for his eminence.'

'To be sure it is. But one thing at a time. There's some gear we'll be needing, and Sainte-Croix is the place to provide it.'

3

They did not, after all, scuttle the Spanish carack, as Captain Blood proposed. The thrifty nature of the little North Country seaman revolted at the thought of such waste, whilst his caution desired to know how he and his hands were ever to get back to England if Blood's schemes should, after all, miscarry even in part and no such tall ship as he promised should be forthcoming.

For the rest, however, the events followed the course that Captain Blood laid down. Steering in a north-easterly direction, the *Arabella,* with the *guarda-costa* following, came a couple of days later to the French settlement of Sainte-Croix, of which the buccaneers were free. Forty-eight hours they remained there, and Captain Blood, with Yberville and the bald-headed little bos'n Snell, who knew his way about every port of the Caribbean, spent most of the time ashore.

Then, leaving the carack to await their return, Walker and his hands transferred themselves to the *Arabella.* She set sail, and laid a westward course once more, in the direction of Puerto Rico. After that she was seen no more until a fortnight later, when her great red hull was sighted off the undulating green hills of the northern coast of Cuba.

In the genial, comparatively temperate airs of that region she sailed along those fertile shores, and so came at last to the entrance of the lagoon on which Havana stood in a majesty of limestone palaces, of churches, monasteries, squares, and market-places that might have been transported bodily from Old Castile to the New World.

Scanning the defences as they approached, Blood realized for himself how little either Walker or Jeremy Pitt had exaggerated their massive strength. The mighty Moro fort, with its sullen bastions and massive towers, occupied a rocky eminence at the very mouth of the channel; opposite to it stood the Puntal, with its demi-lunar batteries; and facing the entrance loomed El Fuerte, no less menacing. Whatever might have been the strength of the place in the time of Drake, he would be rash, indeed, who would run the gantlet of those three formidable guardians now.

The *Arabella* hove-to in the roadstead, announced

herself by firing a gun as a salute, hoisted the Union flag, and awaited events.

They followed soon in the shape of a ten-oared barge, from under the awning of which stepped the Alcalde of the port, Walker's old friend, Don Hieronimo. He puffed his way up the Jacob's-ladder, and came aboard to inquire into the purpose of this ship in these waters.

Captain Blood, in a splendour of purple-and-silver, received him in the waist, attended by Pitt and Wolverstone. A dozen half-naked seamen hovered above the trim decks, and a half-dozen more were aloft clewing up the royals.

Nothing could have exceeded the courtliness with which the Alcalde was made welcome. Blood, who announced himself casually as on his way to Jamaica with a valuable cargo of slaves, had been, he said, constrained by lack of wood and water to put in at Havana. He would depend upon the kindliness and courtesy of the Alcalde for these and also for some fresh victuals for which they would be the better, and he would gladly pay in gold for what they took.

The black-coated Don Hieronimo, pasty-faced and flabby, some five and a half feet high and scarcely less round the belly, with the dewlap of an ox, was not to be seduced by the elegant exterior or courteous phrases of any damned heretical foreigner. He responded coldly, his expression one of consequential malevolence, whilst his shrewd black eyes scoured every corner of those decks suspiciously. Thus until the slaves were mentioned. Then a curious change took place; a measure of affability overspread his forbidding surliness. He went so far as to display his yellow teeth in a smile.

To be sure, the *Señor Capitán* could purchase whatever he required in Havana. To be sure, he was at liberty to enter the port when he pleased, and then not a doubt but that the bumboats would be alongside and able to supply all that he lacked. If not, the Alcalde would be happy to afford him every facility ashore.

Upon these assurances the seaman at the whipstaff was ordered to put down the helm, and Pitt's clear voice rang out in command to the men at the braces, to let go and haul. Catching the breeze again, the *Arabella* crept forward past those formidable forts, with the Alcalde's barge in tow, what time the Alcalde with ever-increasing affability was slyly seeking to draw from Captain Blood some information touching this cargo of slaves in his hold. But so vague and lethargic was Captain Blood upon that subject that in the end Don Hieronimo was forced to come out into the open and deal frankly.

'I may seem persistent in questioning you about these slaves,' he said. 'But that is because it occurs to me that, if you choose, you need not be at the cost of carrying them to Jamaica. You would find a ready market for them here in Havana.'

'In Havana?' Blood raised his eyebrows. 'But is it not against the laws of His Catholic Majesty?'

The Alcalde pursed his thick, dusky lips.

'The law was made when there was no thought for our present difficulties. There has been a scourge of smallpox in the mines, and we are short of hands. Of necessity we must waive the law. If, then, you would care to trade, Sir Captain, there is no obstacle.'

'I see,' said Blood, without enthusiasm.

'And the prices will be good,' added Don Hieronimo, so as to stir him from his lethargy. 'In fact, they will be unusual.'

'So are my slaves. Very unusual.'

'And that's the fact,' Wolverstone confirmed him in his halting Spanish. 'They'll cost you dear, Señor Alcalde. Though I don't suppose ye'll grudge the price when you've had a look at them.'

'If I might see them,' begged the Spaniard.

'Oh, but why not?' was Blood's ready agreement.

The *Arabella* had come by now through the bottleneck into the great blue lagoon that is the Bay of Havana, a full three miles across. The leadsman in the forechains was calling the fathoms, and it occurred to

Blood that it might be prudent to go no farther. He turned aside for a moment, to order Pitt to anchor where they stood, well away from the forest of masts and spars reared by the shipping over against the town. Then he came back to the Alcalde.

'If you will follow me, Don Hieronimo,' said he, and led the way to a scuttle.

By a short, narrow ladder they dropped to the main deck below, where the gloom was shot by shafts of sunlight from the open gun-ports, crossed by others from the gratings overhead. The Alcalde looked along that formidable array of cannon, and at the lines of hammocks slung behind them on either side, in some of which men were even now reposing.

Stooping to avoid the stanchions in that shallow place, he followed his tall leader aft, and was followed in turn by the massive Wolverstone. Presently Blood paused, and turned, to ask a curious question.

'Does it happen, sir, that you are acquainted with the Cardinal-Archbishop Don Ignacio de la Fuente, the new Primate of New Spain?'

'Not yet, sir. He has not yet reached Havana. But we look daily now for the honour of receiving him.'

'It may be yours even sooner than you think.'

'But not sooner than we hope. What, sir, do you know of the Cardinal-Archbishop's voyage?'

Blood, however, had already resumed his progress aft, and did not answer him.

They came at last to the door of the ward-room, which was guarded by two musketeers. A muffled sound of chanting, Gregorian of character, which had mystified the Alcalde as they approached, was now so distinct that, as they halted, he could even distinguish the words of that droned supplication:

> *Hostem repellas longius,*
> *Pacemque dones protinus;*
> *Ductore sic te praevio,*
> *Vitemus omne noxium.*

He frowned, and stared up at Blood.

'*Por Dios!* Are they your slaves who sing?'

'They appear to find consolation in it.'

Don Hieronimo was suspicious without knowing what to suspect. Something here was not as it should be.

'Oddly devout, are they not?' said he.

'Certainly devout. Not oddly.'

At a sign from him one of the musketeers had unbarred the door, and as he now flung it wide, the chanting abruptly broke off on the word *Saeculorum*. The Amen to that hymn was never uttered.

Ceremoniously Blood waved the Alcalde forward. In haste to resolve this riddle, Don Hieronimo stepped boldly and quickly across the threshold, and there abruptly checked, at gaze with horror-stricken, bulging eyes.

In the spacious but sparsely furnished ward-room, invaded by the smell of bilge-water and spun-yarn, and lighted by a window astern, he beheld a dozen figures in the white woollen habit and black cloak of the Order of Saint Dominic. In two rows they sat, silent and immovable as lay-figures, their hands folded within their wide sleeves, their heads bowed and cowled, all save one, who stood uncovered and as if in immediate attendance upon a stately figure that sat apart, enthroned in a tall chair. A tall, handsome man of perhaps forty, he was from head to foot a flame of scarlet. A scarlet skull-cap covered the tonsure to be presumed in his flowing locks of a rich brown that was almost auburn; a collar of finest point adorned the neck of his silken cassock; a gold cross gleamed on his scarlet breast. His very hands were gloved in red, and on the annular finger of his right flashed the episcopal sapphire, worn over his glove. His calm and the austerity in which he was enveloped lent him a dignity of aspect almost superhuman.

His handsome eyes surveyed the gross fellow who had so abruptly and unceremoniously stumbled into that place. But their lofty calm remained unperturbed. It was as if he left human passions to lesser mortals, such as the bareheaded, red-faced, rather bibulous-looking friar behind him, a man, relieved by nature from recourse to the tonsuring razor, whose hairless pate rose brown and gleaming from a crown of grey-greasy curls. A very human brother, this, to judge by the fierce scowl with which he surveyed the intruder.

Forcibly Captain Blood thrust forward the palsied Alcalde, so as to gain room to enter. Hat in hand, he stepped past him some little way, then turned to beckon him forward.

But before he could speak, the Alcalde, apoplectic and out of breath, was demanding to know what this might mean.

Blood was smilingly bland before that indignation.

'Is it not plain? I understand your surprise. But you'll remember that I warned you that my slaves are unusual.'

'Slaves? These?' The Alcalde seemed to choke. 'For sale? In God's name, who are you that you dare so impious, so infernal a jest?'

'I am called Blood, sir. Captain Blood.' And he added, with a bow: 'To serve you.'

'Blood!' The black eyes grew almost invisible in that congested countenance. 'You are Captain Blood? You are that endemonized pirate out of Hell?'

'That is how Spain describes me. But Spain is prejudiced. Leave that, sir, and come.' Again he beckoned him, and what he said confirmed the Alcalde's worst fearful suspicions. 'Let me have the honour of presenting you to His Eminence the Cardinal-Archbishop Don Ignacio de la Fuente, the Primate of New Spain. I told you that it might be yours to welcome him sooner than you thought.'

'God of mercy!' gurgled the Alcalde.

Stately as a court usher, Blood advanced a pace, and bowed low to the Cardinal.

'Eminence, condescend to receive a poor sinner who is, nevertheless, a person of some consequence in these parts: the Alcalde of the Port of Havana.'

At the same moment Don Hieronimo was thrust violently forward by the Herculean arm of Wolverstone, who bawled after him: 'On your knees, sir, to ask a blessing of his eminence.'

The prelate's calm, inscrutable, deep-set eyes were considering the horrified officer who was now on his knees before him.

'Eminence!' gasped Don Hieronimo, almost in tears. 'Eminence!'

As steady as the glance was the deep, rich voice that murmured, *'Pax tibi, filius meus,'* whilst in slow majesty the hand that bore the cardinalitial ring was extended to be kissed.

Faltering 'Eminence' yet again, the Alcalde fell upon it and bore it to his mouth as if he would eat it.

'What horror!' he wailed. 'My God, what horror! What sacrilege!'

A smile infinitely wistful, infinitely compassionate and saintly broke upon the prelate's handsome face.

'We offer up these ills for our sins, my son, thankful, since that is so, that they are given us to endure. We are for sale, it seems, I and these poor brethren of Saint Dominic who accompany me and share my duress at the hands of our heretical captors. We must pray for grace to bear it with becoming fortitude, remembering that those great Apostles, Saint Peter and Saint Paul, also suffered incarceration in the fulfilment of their sacred missions.'

Don Hieronimo was scrambling to his feet, moving sluggishly, not only from his obesity, but also from overpowering emotion.

'But how could such a horror come to pass?' he groaned.

'Let it not distress you, my son, that I should be a prisoner in the hands of this poor, blind heretic.'

'Three errors in three words, Eminence,' was Blood's comment. 'Behold how easy is error, and let it serve as a warning against hasty judgments when you are called upon to judge, as presently you shall be. I am not poor.

I am not blind. I am not a heretic. I am a true son of Mother Church. And if I have reluctantly laid violent hands upon your eminence, it was not only so that you might be a hostage for the righting of a monstrous wrong that has been done in the name of the Catholic King and the Holy Faith, but so that in your wisdom and piety you might yourself deliver judgment upon the deed and the doer.'

Through his teeth the bareheaded, red-faced little friar, leaning forward and snarling like a terrier, uttered three words of condemnation.

'*Perro hereje maldito!*'

Instantly the Cardinal's gloved hand was raised imperiously to rebuke and restrain him.

'Peace, Frey Domingo!

'I spoke, sir, of poverty and blindness of the spirit, not of the flesh,' he quietly answered Blood, and continued, addressing him in the second person singular, as if more signally to mark the gulf between them: 'For in that sense poor and blind thou art.' He sighed. More sternly still he added: 'That thou shouldst confess thyself a son of the True Church is but to confess this outrage more scandalous than I had supposed it.'

'Suspend your judgment, Eminence, until all my motive is disclosed,' said Blood, and, taking a step or two in the direction of the open door, he raised his voice to call, 'Captain Walker!'

In answer, a bow-legged, red-haired little man, all fire and truculence, advanced with a rolling gait to nod curtly to the scarlet presence, and then, arms akimbo, to confront the Alcalde.

'Good day to you, Don Ladrón, which is what I calls you. You'ld not be expecting to see me again so soon, ye murdering villain. Ye didna know, maybe, that an English sailor has as many lives as a cat. I've come back for my hides, ye thief. My hides, and my tall ship as your rascals sank under me.'

If anything at that moment could have added to the Alcalde's distress and rage and to the confusion of his wits, this reappearance of Captain Walker certainly supplied it. Yellow-faced and shaking from head to foot, he stood gasping and mouthing, desperately seeking words in which to answer. But Captain Blood gave him little time to strain his wits.

'So now, Don Hieronimo, perhaps you begin to understand,' he said.

'We are here in quest of restitution of what was stolen, of reparation for a crime. And for this his eminence there is no more than a hostage in our hands.

'I will not trouble you to restore the hides out of which you and your Captain-General between you swindled this poor seaman. But you'll pay in gold the price they would have fetched in England; that is twenty thousand pieces of eight. And you'll provide a ship of a burthen at least equal to that which your *guarda-costa* sank by orders of your Captain-General, this ship to be of not less than twenty guns, all found, armed, and victualled for a voyage. Time enough, when that is done, to discuss putting his eminence ashore.'

There was a streak of blood on the Alcalde's chin, from the wound his teeth had made in his lip. Yet frenzied, though he might be by impotent rage, yet he was not so blinded but that he perceived that the guns of the mighty forts of Havana, and of the Admiral's squadron within range of which this private vessel impudently rode at anchor, were powerless against her whilst the sacred person of the Primate of New Spain was in her hold. Similarly to attempt to take her by assault must be fraught by a like deadly peril for the Cardinal at the hands of men so desperate and bloody as these. At whatever cost, his eminence must be delivered, and this with the least delay. In all the circumstances it was perhaps a matter for thankfulness that the pirate's demands should be as modest as they were.

He strove for dignity, drew himself up and thrust out his paunch, and spoke to Blood in the tone of a man addressing his lackey.

'I do not parley with you. I will inform his excellency

the Captain-General.' He turned to the Cardinal, with a change to utmost humility. 'Give me leave, Eminence, accepting my assurance that you will not be allowed to remain in this scandalous duress one moment longer than may be unavoidable. Give me leave.'

He bowed very low, and would have withdrawn. But the Cardinal gave him no such leave just yet. He had been listening with obvious attention to what passed.

'Wait, sir. Wait. There is something here that I do not understand.' A puzzled frown stood between his brows. 'This man speaks of restitution, of reparation. Has he the right to use such words?'

It was Blood who answered him.

'I desire your eminence to be the judge of that. That is the judgment to which I alluded. It is so that you may deliver it that I have ventured to lay hands upon your sacred person, for which I shall hope for your absolution in the end.' Thereupon, in a dozen crisp, incisive sentences, he sketched the tale of the robbery of Captain Walker under the cloak of legal justification.

When he had done, the Cardinal looked at him with scorn, and from him turned to the fuming Alcalde. His gentle voice was warm with indignation.

'That tale, of course, is false. Impossible. It does not deceive me. No Castilian man of honour placed by His Catholic Majesty in authority could be guilty of such turpitude. You hear, Sir Alcalde, how this misguided pirate imperils his immortal soul by bearing false witness.'

The perspiring Alcalde's answer did not come as promptly as his eminence expected it.

'But is it possible that you hesitate?' he asked, as if startled, leaning forward.

Desperately Don Hieronimo broke into stumbling speech.

'It is that . . . *Dios mio!* The tale is grossly exaggerated. It . . .'

'Exaggerated!' The gentle voice was suddenly and sharply raised. 'Exaggerated? Not wholly false, then?'

The only answer he received was a cringing hunch of the Alcalde's shoulders and a glance that fell in fear under the prelate's stern eyes.

The Cardinal-Archbishop sank back into his chair, his face inscrutable, his voice of an ominous quiet.

'You have leave to go. You will request the Captain-General of Havana to wait upon me here in person. I require to know more of this.'

'He . . . he may require safe-conduct,' stuttered the unfortunate Alcalde.

'It is granted him.' said Captain Blood.

'You hear? I shall expect him at the earliest.' And the scarlet hand with its sapphire ring majestically waved Don Hieronimo away.

Daring no more, the Alcalde bowed himself double, and went out backwards as if from a royal presence.

4

If the tale borne by Don Hieronimo to the Captain-General, of Captain Blood's outrageous and sacrilegious violence to the Cardinal-Archbishop of New Spain filled Don Ruiz with amazement, dismay, and horrified indignation, the summons on which it concluded, and the reasons for it, supplied a stimulus that presently moved his excellency to almost superhuman activity. If he delayed four hours in answering in person that summons, at least the answer that he then delivered was of such a fullness that it would have taken an ordinary Spaniard in ordinary circumstances as many days to have prepared it.

His conscience shaken into uneasiness by what his subordinate told him, Don Ruiz Perera de Valdoro y Peñascon, who was also Count of Marcos, deemed it well to omit in the Cardinal-Archbishop's service no effort that might be calculated to conciliate his eminence. It occurred to him, naturally enough, that nothing could be more conciliatory, nothing would be more likely to put the Cardinal in a good humour with him than if he were to present himself in the rôle of his eminence's immediate deliverer from the hands of that abominable pirate who held him captive.

Therefore, by exertions unprecedented in all his experience Don Ruiz so contrived that in seeking the Cardinal-Archbishop, aboard the *Arabella,* he was actually able to fulfil all the conditions upon which he understood that Captain Blood had consented to restore his prisoner to liberty. So great an achievement must fill the Primate with a wonder and gratitude that would leave no room for petty matters.

Thus, then, it fell out almost incredibly that when, some four hours after the Alcalde's departure from the *Arabella,* the Captain-General came alongside in his barge, a broad-beamed, two-masted, square-rigged brigantine was warped to a station a cable's length from the buccaneer's larboard quarter. In addition to this, Don Ruiz, who climbed the ladder with the Alcalde in close attendance, was followed by two *alguaziles,* each of whom shouldered a wooden coffer of some weight.

Captain Blood had taken his precautions against treachery. His gun-ports had been opened on the larboard side, and twenty threatening muzzles had been run out. As his excellency stepped down into the waist, his contemptuous eyes saw the bulwarks lined by men, some half-naked, some fully clothed, and some actually in armour; but all with muskets poised and matches glowing.

A tall, narrow-faced gentleman with a bold nose, Don Ruiz came dressed as was demanded by an occasion of such ceremony. He was magnificent in gold-laced black. He wore the cross of Saint James on his breast, and a gold-hilted sword swung at his side. He carried a long cane in one hand and a gold-edged handkerchief in the other.

Under his little black moustaches his thin lips curled in disdain as he acknowledged the bow with which Captain Blood received him. The deepening sallowness of his face bore witness to the wicked humour upon which he strove to set that mask of lofty contempt.

He delivered himself without preamble.

'Your impudent conditions are fulfilled, sir pirate. There is the ship you have demanded, and here in these coffers is the gold; the twenty thousand pieces. It is now for you to keep your part of the bargain struck, and so make an end of the sacrilegious infamy of which you have been guilty.'

Without answering him, Captain Blood turned and beckoned forward the little North-Country shipmaster from the background, where he stood glowering at Don Ruiz.

'You hear, Captain Walker.' He pointed to the coffers, which the *alguaziles* had set down upon the hatch-coaming. 'There, says his excellency, is your gold. Verify it, then take it, put your men aboard that brigantine, spread your sails, and be off whilst I am still here to make your departure safe.'

For a moment amazement and emotion before such munificence rendered the little slaver dumb. Then speech bubbled out of him in a maudlin gush of wonder and gratitude which Blood made haste to stem.

'It's wasting good time ye are, my friend. Sure, don't I know all that: that I'm great and noble and that it was the lucky day for you when I put a shot athwart your hawse? Away with you now, and say a good word for Peter Blood in England when ye get there.'

'But this gold,' Walker still protested. 'Ye'll take the half of it at least?'

'Och, now! What's a trifle of gold? I'll know how to repay myself for my trouble, ye may be sure. Gather your hands and be off, and God be with you, my friend.'

When at last he had wrenched his fingers from the crushing grip into which the slaver packed all the emotion that he could not properly utter, Blood gave his attention to Don Ruiz, who had stood aloof with the Alcalde, disdainful of eye and lip.

'If you will follow me, I will conduct you to his eminence.'

He led the way below, and Pitt and Wolverstone went with them.

In the ward-room, at sight of that majestic figure, glittering in scarlet splendour against the humble monkish background, Don Ruiz, with an inarticulate cry, ran forward to cast himself upon his knees.

'*Benedictus sis,*' murmured the Primate, and gave him his ring to kiss.

'My lord! Eminence! That these incarnate devils should have subjected your saintliness to such indignity!'

'That is not important, my son,' said the gentle, musical voice. 'By me and these my brethren in Christ suffering is accepted thankfully, as something of which to make an offering to the Throne of Grace. What is important, what gives me deep concern, is the reason pretexted for it, which I learned only this morning here. I have been told, Lord Count, that in the King's name delivery was refused of merchandise that had been sold to an English seaman; that the moneys he had already paid, as the price of that merchandise, were confiscated; that he was driven empty away with threats of prosecution by the Holy Office; and that even when, thus robbed, he had departed, his ship was pursued and sunk by one of your *guarda-costas*.

'These things I have heard, my son; but although your Alcalde did not contradict them, I must refuse to believe that a gentleman of Spain and a representative of His Catholic Majesty in these parts could be guilty of such conduct.'

Don Ruiz got to his feet. Sallower than ever was his narrow face. But he contrived that his tone should be easy and his manner imposing. By a certain loftiness he hoped to wave the matter away.

'That is all overpast, Eminence. If error there was, it has now been corrected, and with generous interest, as this buccaneer captain will bear me witness. I am here

to give myself the honour of escorting your eminence
ashore to the joyous welcome that awaits you and the
great reception which expectant Havana has been preparing for some weeks.'

But his ingratiatory smile found no reflection in the
Primate's lofty countenance. It remained overcast, sadly grave.

'Ah! You admit the error, then. But you do not explain it.'

Choleric by nature and imperious from long habit of
command, the Captain-General was momentarily in
danger of forgetting that he stood in the presence of
one who was virtually the Pope of the New World, a
man whose powers there were inferior only to the
King's, and before whom in certain matters even the
King himself must bow. Although he remembered it in
time, a hint of tartness still invested his reply.

'Explanation must prove tedious to your eminence,
and perhaps obscure, since these are matters concerned
with my legal office. Your eminence's great and re-
nowned enlightenment will scarcely cover what is a matter of jurisprudence.'

The most wistful of smiles broke upon that handsome
face.

'You are indifferently informed, I fear, Don Ruiz.
You can never have heard that I have held the exalted
office of Grand Inquisitor of Castile, or you would
know—since it must follow—that I am doctor, not only
of canon, but of civil law. Be under no apprehension,
then, that I shall fail to follow your legal exposition of
the event, and even less on the score of tedium. Many of
my duties are tedious, my son; but they are not on that
account avoided.'

To that cold, relentless insistence the Captain-General saw himself under the necessity of submitting. He
swallowed his annoyance, steadied himself, and provided himself with a scapegoat who would not dare, on
his life, to deny him.

'In brief, Eminence, these transactions were permitted without my knowledge by my Alcalde.' The au-

dible gasp from Don Hieronimo, who stood behind him, did not deter his excellency. He went steadily on. 'When I learned of them, I had no choice but to cancel them, since it is my duty to insist upon the law which forbids all foreigners to trade in His Catholic Majesty's dominions.'

'With that there could be no quarrel. But I understand that this English seaman had already paid for the merchandise.'

'He had traded slaves for them, Eminence.'

'No matter what he had traded. Were his slaves restored to him when the transaction was cancelled by you?'

'The laws which he defied when he traded them decreed their confiscation likewise.'

'Ordinarily that might be so. But this, if I am rightly informed, is no ordinary case. I am told that he was urged to trade his slaves by your Alcalde.'

'Just as I,' Blood interposed, 'was urged by him this morning to trade mine.' And the sweep of his hand indicated the Cardinal-Archbishop and his attendant monks. 'He does not learn by his errors, then, this Alcalde of yours. Perhaps you do not desire that he shall.'

Ostentatiously Don Ruiz turned his shoulder upon Blood, ignoring him.

'Your eminence cannot account me bound by the illegality of a subordinate.' Then, permitting himself a little smile, he added the sophism which he had already used with Captain Walker. 'If a man commit murder, it cannot exculpate him to say that he had the sanction of another.'

'That is to be subtle, is it not? I must take thought upon this, Don Ruiz. We will talk of it again.'

Don Ruiz bowed low, his lip in his teeth.

'At your eminence's disposal,' he said. 'Meanwhile, my barge is waiting to carry your eminence ashore.'

The Cardinal rose, imposingly tall in his robes, and drew his scarlet cloak about him. The cowled Dominicans, who had stood like statues, stirred responsively into life. His eminence turned to them.

'Be mindful, my children, to return thanks for this safe deliverance. Let us go.'

And he stepped forward, to be checked at once by Captain Blood.

'Patience yet awhile, Eminence. All is not done.'

The Cardinal threw up his head, a frown darkening his brow.

'How? What, then, remains?'

Blood's answer was delivered rather to the scowling Captain-General than to the prelate.

'So far we have had no more than restitution. Come we now to the question of compensations.'

'Compensations!' cried the Primate, and for once the splendid calm of him was ruffled. Sternly he added the questions: 'What is this? Do you break faith, sir?'

'That, at least, has never yet been said of me. I break no faith. On the contrary, I am punctilious. What I told the Alcalde was that when restitution was made, we would discuss the matter of your eminence's landing. That we would discuss it. No more than that.'

Don Ruiz smiled in rage and malice, a smile that displayed his white teeth.

'Ingenious. Yes. And then, you brigand?'

'I could not, without disrespect to his eminence the Primate of New Spain, set his ransom at less than a hundred thouand ducats.'

Don Ruiz sucked in his breath. He went livid. His jaw fell loose.

'A hundred thousand ducats!'

'That is today. Tomorrow I may not be so modest.'

The Captain-General in his fury swung to the Cardinal, his gestures wild.

'Your eminence hears what this thief now demands?'

But the Cardinal, having now resumed his unworldly calm, was not again to be shaken from it.

'Patience, my son. Patience! Let us beware the mortal sin of anger, which will scarcely hasten my release for the Apostolic labours that await me in Havana.'

It would have needed a great deal more than this to bring Don Ruiz to yield had not the very fury that now possessed him, craving an orgy of vengeance, shown him the way. Trembling a little in his suppressed wrath, yet he was sufficiently master of himself to bow as if to an order, and to promise in comparatively civil terms that the money should at once be forthcoming, in order that his eminence's deliverance should be procured at the earliest moment.

5

But in his barge, as he was returning to shore with the Alcalde, the Captain-General betrayed the fact that it was not the deliverance of the Cardinal-Archbishop that spurred him so much as his eagerness to crush this impudent pirate who defeated him at his own game.

'The fool shall have the gold, so that destruction may overtake him.'

Gloomily the Alcalde shook his head.

'It's a terrible price to pay. God of my life! A hundred thousand pieces!'

'There's no help for that.' Almost Don Ruiz implied by his manner that he accounted cheap at the price the destruction of a man who had brought him to such humiliation that he, the Captain-General of Havana, lord of life and death in those parts, had been made to look no better than a schoolboy standing to be birched. 'Nor is it so exorbitant. The Admiral of the Ocean-Sea is willing to pay fifty thousand pieces for the head of Captain Blood. I but double it—out of the Royal Treasury.'

'But what the Marquis of Riconete pays would not be lost. Whilst this will be sunk with that scoundrel.'

'But perhaps not beyond recovery. It depends upon where we sink him. Where he's anchored now, there's not above four fathoms, and it's all shallow on that side as far as the bar. But that's no matter. What matters is to get the Cardinal-Archbishop out of that ship, so as to put an end to its cursed immunity.'

'Are you so sure that it will end then? That sly devil will demand pledges, oaths.'

Don Ruiz laughed savagely from livid lips.

'He shall have them. All the pledges, all the oaths, that he requires. An oath sworn under constraint has never been accounted binding on any man.'

But the Alcalde's gloom was not relieved.

'That will not be his eminence's view.'

'His eminence?'

'Can you doubt that this damned pirate will ask a pledge from him—a pledge of safe-conduct for himself? You've seen the man this Cardinal is: a narrow, bigoted zealot, a slave to the letter of a contract. It's an ill thing to set up priests as judges. They're so unfitted for the office. There's no humanity in them, no breadth of understanding. What this prelate swears, that he will do, no matter where or how the oath may have been exacted.'

For a moment dismay darkened still further the Captain-General's soul. A little thought, however, and his tortuous mind had found a way. He laughed again.

'I thank you, Don Hieronimo, for that forewarning. I am not pledged yet, nor will those be upon whom I shall depend, and who shall have my instant orders.'

Back in his palace, before coming to the matter of the Cardinal's ransom, he summoned one of his officers.

'The Cardinal-Archbishop of New Spain will land this evening at Havana,' he announced. 'To do him honour, and so that the city may be apprised of this happy event, I shall require a salute to be fired from the gun on the mole. You will take a gunner and station yourself there. The moment his eminence sets foot on land you will order the gun to be touched off.'

On that he dismissed the officer and summoned another one.

'You will take horse at once and ride to El Fuerte, to the Moro, and the Puntal. In my name you will order the commandant of each of those forts to train his guns on that red ship at anchor yonder, flying the English flag. After that they are to wait for the signal, which will be the firing of the gun on the mole when the Cardinal-Archbishop of New Spain comes ashore. As soon as they hear it, but not before, they are to open fire upon that pirate ship and sink her. Let there be no mistake.'

Upon the officer's assurance that all was perfectly clear, Don Ruiz dismissed him to carry those orders, and then turned his attention to raiding the Royal Treasury for the gold which was to deliver the Cardinal from his duress.

So expeditiously did he go about this matter that he was alongside the *Arabella* again by the first dog-watch, and out of his barge four massive chests were hoisted to the deck of the buccaneer.

It had enheartened both him and the Alcalde, who again faithfully accompanied him, to behold, as they approached, the Cardinal-Archbishop on the poop-deck. Mantled and red-hatted, his crozier borne before him by the bareheaded Frey Domingo, and the other Dominicans modestly cowled and ranged behind him, it was clear that already his eminence was ready and waiting to go ashore. This, and the measure of liberty which his presence on deck announced had already been accorded to him, finally assured Don Ruiz that once the ransom was paid there would be an end of the sacrilege of his eminence's detention and no further obstacle would delay his departure from that accursed ship. With the removal of that protecting consecrated presence, the immunity of the *Arabella* would be at an end, and the guns of the Havana forts would make short work of her timbers.

Exulting in this thought, Don Ruiz could not refrain from taking with Blood, who received him at the head of the entrance ladder, the tone proper from a royal representative to a pirate.

'*Maldito ladrón*—accursed thief—there is your gold,

the price of a sacrilege for which you'll burn in Hell through all eternity. Verify it, and let us begone.'

Captain Blood gave no hint that he was so much as touched by that insulting speech. He stooped to the massive chests, unlocked each in turn and cast a casual yet appraising glance over the gleaming contents. Then he beckoned his shipmaster forward.

'Jerry, here is the gold. See it stowed.' Almost disdainfully he added: 'We assume the count to be correct.'

Thereupon he turned to the poop and to the scarlet figure at the rail, and raised his voice.

'My Lord Cardinal, the ransom has been received and the Captain-General's barge waits to take you ashore. You have but to pledge me your word that I shall be allowed to depart without let, hindrance, or pursuit.'

Under his little black moustaches the Captain-General's lip curled in a little smile. The slyness of the man displays itself in the terms, so calculated to avert suspicion, in which he chose to give expression to his venom.

'You may depart now without let or hindrance, you rogue. But if ever we meet again upon the seas, as meet we shall . . .'

He left his sentence there. But Captain Blood completed it for him.

'It is probable that I shall have the satisfaction of hanging you from that yardarm, like the forsworn, dishonoured thief you are, you gentleman of Spain.'

At the head of the companion the advancing Cardinal paused to reprove him for those words.

'Captain Blood, that threat is as ungenerous as I hope the terms of it are untrue.'

Don Ruiz caught his breath, aghast, more enraged even by the reproof than by the offensive terms of the threat that had provoked it.

'You hope!' he cried. 'Your eminence hopes!'

'Wait!' Slowly the Cardinal descended the steps of the companion, his monks following him, and came to stand in the waist, a very incarnation of the illimitable power and majesty of the Church.

'I said I hoped that the accusation is untrue, and that implies a doubt, which has offended you. For that doubt, Don Ruiz, I shall hope presently to seek your pardon. But first, since last you were here something has been troubling me which I must ask you to resolve.'

'Ashore, your eminence will find me ready fully to answer your every question.' And Don Ruiz strode away to place himself at the head of the ladder by which the Cardinal was to descend. Captain Blood at the same moment, hat in hand, passed to its other side and took up his station there, as the courteous speeding of a departing guest demanded.

But the Primate did not move from where he stood.

'Don Ruiz, there is one question that must be answered before I consent to land in a province that you govern.' And so stern and commanding was his mien that Don Ruiz, at whose nod a population trembled, stood in dismay before him, waiting.

The Cardinal's glance passed from him to the attendant Don Hieronimo, and it was to him that the crucial question was set.

'Señor Alcalde, weigh well your answer to me, for your office and perhaps even more will depend upon your accuracy. What was done with the merchandise —the property of that English seaman—which the Captain-General ordered you to confiscate?'

Don Hieronimo's uneasy eyes looked anywhere but at his questioner. Intimidated, he dared not be other than prompt and truthful in his reply.

'It was sold again, Eminence.'

'And the gold it fetched? What became of that?'

'I delivered it to his excellency the Captain-General. Some twelve thousand ducats.'

In the hushed pause that followed, Don Ruiz bore the searching scrutiny of those stern, sad eyes, with his head high and a scornful, defiant curl to his lip. But the

Primate's next question wiped the last vestige of that arrogance from his countenance.

'And is, then, the Captain-General of Havana also the King's Treasurer?'

'Not so, of course, Eminence,' said Don Ruiz, perforce.

'Then, sir, did you in your turn surrender to the treasury this gold received for goods you confiscated in the name of the King your master?'

He dared not prevaricate where verification of his word must so shortly follow. His tone, nevertheless, was surly with resentment of such a question.

'Not yet, Eminence. But . . .'

'Not yet!' The Cardinal allowed him to go no further, and there was an undertone of thunder in that gentle, interrupting voice. 'Not yet? And it is a full month since those events. I am answered, sir. Unhappily I did you no wrong by my doubt, which was that an officer of the Crown who interprets the laws with such sophistries as that which you uttered to me this morning cannot possibly be honest.'

'Eminence!' It was a roar of anger. In his excitement, his face livid, he advanced a step. Such words wherever uttered to him must have moved his wrath. But to be admonished and insulted by this priest in public, to be held up to the scorn and derision of these ruffianly buccaneers, was something beyond the endurance of any Castilian gentleman. In his fury he was seeking words in which to answer the indignity as it deserved, when, as if divining his mind, the Primate launched a scornful fulmination that withered his anger, and turned it into fear.

'Silence, man! Will you raise your voice to us? By such means as these you no doubt grow rich in gold, but still richer in dishonour. And there is more. So that this unfortunate English seaman should quietly suffer himself to be robbed, you threatened him with prosecution by the Holy Office and the fires of the Faith. Even a New Christian, and a New Christian more than any other, should know that to invoke the Holy Office for such base ends is to bring himself within the scope of its just resentment.'

That terrible threat on the lips of a sometime Grand Inquisitor, and the terms in which it was delivered, with its hint of Old Christian scorn of New Christian blood, was the lightning-stroke that reduced the Captain-General's heart to ashes. He stood appalled, in fancy already seeing himself dishonoured, ruined, sent home to be arraigned in an *auto-da-fé,* stripped of every dignity before being deprived of life itself.

'My lord!' It was the piteous wail of a broken man. He held out hands in supplication. 'I did not see . . .'

'That I can well believe. *Oculos habent et non videbunt.* No man who saw would incur that peril.'

Then his normal calm descended upon him again. Awhile he stood thoughtful and about him all was respectful silence. Then he sighed, and advanced to take the stricken Count of Marcos by the arm. He led him away towards the forecastle, out of earshot of the others. He spoke very gently.

'Believe me, my heart bleeds for you, my son. *Humanum est errare.* Sinners are we all. I practise mercy where I can, against my own need of mercy. Therefore, the little that I can do to help you, I will do. Once I am ashore in Cuba, whilst you are its Captain-General I must discover it to be my clear duty as Inquisitor of the Faith to take action in this matter. And that action of necessity must break you. To avoid this, my son, I will not land whilst you hold office here. But this is the utmost that I can do. Perhaps even in doing so much, I am guilty of a sophistry myself. But I have to think not only of you, but also of the proud Castilian name and the honour of Spain herself, which must suffer in the dishonour of one of her administrators. At the same time you will see that I cannot suffer that one who has so grossly abused the King's trust should continue in authority, or that his offence should go entirely unpunished.'

He paused a moment, whilst Don Ruiz stood in abjection with lowered head to hear the sentence that he knew must follow.

'You will resign your governorship this very day, on any pretext that you choose, and you will take the first ship for Spain. Then, so long as you do not return to the New World or assume any public office at home, so long shall I avoid official knowledge of your offence. More I cannot do. And may God forgive me if already I do too much.'

If the sentence was harsh, yet the broken man who listened heard it almost in relief, for he had not dared to expect to be so lightly quit.

'So be it, Eminence,' he faltered, his head still bowed. Then he raised eyes of despair and bewilderment to meet the Cardinal's compassionate eyes. 'But if your eminence does not land . . . ?'

'Do not be concerned for me. I have already sounded this Captain Blood against my possible need. Now that I have taken my resolve, he shall carry me to San Domingo. Thence I can take ship to return here to Havana, and by that time you will have departed.'

Thus Don Ruiz saw himself cheated even of his vengeance upon that accursed sea-robber who had brought this ruin upon him. He began a last, weak, despairing attempt to avert at least that.

'But will you trust these pirates, who already have . . . ?'

He was interrupted.

'In this world, my son, I have learnt to place my trust in Heaven rather than in man. And this buccaneer, for all the evil in him, is a son of the True Church, and he has shown me that he is a scrupulous observer of his word. If there are risks I must accept them. See to it by your future conduct that I accept them in a good cause. Now go with God, Don Ruiz. There is no reason why I should detain you longer.'

The Captain-General went down on his knees to kiss

the Cardinal's ring and ask a blessing. Over his bowed
head the Primate of New Spain extended his right hand,
two fingers and the thumb extended, and made the Sign
of the Cross.

'*Benedictus sis. Pax Domini sit semper tecum.* May
the light of grace show you better ways in future. Depart with God.'

But for all the penitence displayed in his attitude at
the Cardinal's feet, it is to be doubted if he departed as
admonished. Stumbling like a blind man to the entrance
ladder, with a curt summons to the Alcalde to attend
him and not so much as a glance or word to anybody
else, he went over the side and down to his waiting
barge.

And whilst he and the Alcalde raged in mutual sympathy, and damned the Cardinal-Archbishop for a vain,
meddling priest, the *Arabella* was weighing anchor.
Under full sail she swaggered past the massive forts and
out of the Bay of Havana, safe from molestation, since
because of the imposing scarlet figure that paced the
poop the signal gun could not be fired.

And that is how it came to pass that when a fortnight later that great galleon the *Santa Veronica*, in a
bravery of flags and pennants and with guns thunder-
ing in salute, sailed into the Bay of Havana, there was
no Captain-General to welcome the arriving Primate of
New Spain. To deepen the annoyance of that short, corpulent, choleric little prelate, not only was there no
proper preparation for his welcome, but the Alcalde,
who came aboard in an anguish of bewilderment, was
within an ace of treating his eminence as an impostor.

Aboard the *Arabella* in those days, Yberville, di-
vested of his scarlet splendours, which, like the monkish
gowns, had been hurriedly procured in Sainte-Croix,
was giving himself airs and vowing that a great churchman had been lost to the world when he became a buccaneer. Captain Blood, however, would concede no

more than that the loss was that of a great comedian. And in this the bos'n Snell, whom nature had so suitably tonsured for the part of Frey Domingo, being a heretic, entirely concurred with Captain Blood.

6

✦

The Eloping Hidalga

1

WORD WAS BROUGHT to Tortuga by a half-caste Indian
who had shipped as one of the hands on a French brig,
of the affair in which the unfortunate James Sherarton
lost his life. It was a nasty story, with which we are only
indirectly concerned here, so that it need be no more
than briefly stated. Sherarton and the party of English
pearl-fishers he directed were at work off one of the
Espada Keys near the Gulf of Maracaybo. They had
already garnered a considerable harvest, when a Spanish
frigate came upon them, and, not content with seizing
their sloop and their pearls, ruthlessly put them to the
sword. And there were twelve of them, honest, decent
men who were breaking no laws from any but the Spanish point of view, which would admit no right of any
other nation in the waters of the New World.

Captain Blood was present in the Tavern of the King
of France at Cayona when the half-caste told in nau-
seous detail the story of that massacre.

'Spain shall pay,' he said. And his sense of justice
being poetic, he added: 'And she shall pay in pearls.'

Beyond that he gave no hint of the intention which
had leapt instantly to his mind. The inspiration was as
natural as it was sudden. The very mention of pearl-
fisheries had been enough to call to his mind the Rio
de La Hacha, that most productive of all the pearl-
fisheries in the Caribbean from which such treasures
were brought to the surface, to the profit of King Philip.

It was not the first time that the notion of raiding that

162

source of Spanish wealth had occurred to him; but the difficulties and dangers with which the enterprise was fraught had led him hitherto to postpone it in favour of some easier immediate task. Never, however, had those difficulties and dangers been heavier than at this moment, when it almost seemed that the task was imposed upon him by a righteously indignant Nemesis. He was not blind to this. He knew how fiercely vigilant was the Spanish Admiral of the Ocean-Sea, the Marquis of Riconete, who was cruising with a powerful squadron off the Main. So rudely had Captain Blood handled him in that affair at San Domingo that the Admiral dared not show himself again in Spain until he had wiped out the disgrace of it. The depth of his vindictiveness might be gauged from the announcement, which he had published far and wide, that he would pay the enormous sum of fifty thousand pieces of eight for the person of Captain Blood, dead or alive, or for information that should result in his capture.

If, then, a raid on Rio de La Hacha were to succeed, it was of the first importance that it should be carried out smoothly and swiftly. The buccaneers must be away with their plunder before the Admiral could even suspect their presence off the coast. With a view to making sure of this, Captain Blood took the resolve of first reconnoitering the ground in person, and rendering himself familiar with its every detail, so that there should be no fumbling when the raid took place.

Moulting his normal courtly plumage, discarding gold lace and Mechlin, he dissembled his long person in brown homespun, woollen stockings, plain linen bands, and a hat without adornment. He discarded his periwig, and replaced it by a kerchief of black silk that swathed his cropped head like a skull-cap.

In this guise, leaving at Tortuga his fleet, which consisted in those days of four ships manned by close upon a thousand buccaneers, he sailed alone for Curaçao in a trading vessel, and there transferred himself to a broad-beamed Dutchman, the *Loewen,* that made regular voyages to and fro between that island and Cartagena. He represented himself as a trader in hides and the like, and assumed the name of Tormillo and a mixed Dutch and Spanish origin.

It was on a Monday that he landed from the Dutchman at Rio de La Hacha. The *Loewen* would be back from Cartagena on the following Friday, and even if no other business should bring her to Rio de La Hacha, she would call there again so as to pick up Señor Tormillo, who would be returning in her to Curaçao. He had contrived, largely at the cost of drinking too much bumbo, to establish the friendliest relations with the Dutch skipper, so as to ensure the faithful observance of this arrangement.

Having been put ashore by the Dutchman's cockboat, he took lodgings at the Escudo de León, a decent inn in the upper part of the town, and gave out that he was in Rio de La Hacha to purchase hides. Soon the traders flocked to him and he won their esteem by the quantity of hides he agreed to purchase, and their amused contempt by the liberal prices he agreed to pay. In the pursuit of his business he went freely and widely about the place, and in the intervals between purchases he contrived to observe what was to be observed and to collect the information that he required.

So well did he employ his time that by the evening of Thursday he had fully accomplished all that he came to do. He was acquainted with the exact armament and condition of the fort that guarded the harbour, with the extent and quality of the military establishment, with the situation and defences of the royal treasury, where the harvest of pearls was stored; he had even contrived to inspect the fishery where the pearling boats were at work under the protection of a ten-gun *guarda-costa;* and he had ascertained that the Marquis of Riconete, having flung out swift scouting vessels, had taken up his headquarters at Cartagena, a hundred and fifty miles away, to the southwest. Not only this, but he had fully evolved in his mind the plan by which the Spanish scouts were to be eluded and the place surprised, so that it might quickly be cleaned up before the Admiral's squadron could supervene to hinder.

Content, he came back to the Escudo de León on that Thursday evening for his last night in his lodging there. In the morning the Dutchman should be back to take him off again, his mission smoothly accomplished. And then that happened which altered everything and was destined to change the lives and fortunes of persons of whose existence at that hour he was not even aware.

The landlord met him with the news that a Spanish gentleman, Don Francisco de Villamarga, had just been seeking him at the inn, and would return again in an hour's time. The mention of that name seemed suddenly to diminish the stifling heat of the evening for him. But, at least, he kept his breath and his countenance.

'Don Francisco de Villamarga?' he slowly repeated, giving himself time to thing. Was it possible that there were in the New World two Spaniards of that same distinguished name? 'I seem to remember that a Don Francisco de Villamarga was Deputy-Governor of Maracaybo.'

'It is the same, sir,' the landlord answered him. 'Don Francisco was Governor there, or, at least, Alcalde, until about a year ago.'

'And he asked for me?'

'For you, Señor Tormillo. He came back from the interior today, he says, with a parcel of green hides which he desires to offer you.'

'Oh!' It was almost a gasp of relief. The Captain breathed more freely, but not yet freely enough. 'Don Francisco with hides to sell? Don Francisco de Villamarga a trader?'

The fat little vintner spread his hands.

'What would you, sir? This is the New World. Here such things can happen to a *hidalgo* when he is not fortunate. And Don Francisco, poor gentleman, has had sad misfortune, through no fault of his own. The province of his governorship was raided by Captain Blood, that accursed pirate, and Don Francisco fell into disgrace. What would you? It is the way of these things.

There is no mercy for a governor who cannot protect a place entrusted to him.'

'I see.' Captain Blood took off his broad hat, and mopped his brow that was beaded with sweat below the line of the black scarf.

So far all was well, thanks to the fortunate chance of his absence when Don Francisco had called. But the danger of recognition, which so far had been safely run, was now only just round the corner. And there were few men in New Spain by whom Captain Blood would be more reluctant to be recognized than by this sometime Deputy-Governor of Maracaybo, this proud Spanish gentleman who had been constrained, for the reasons given by the innkeeper, to soil his hands in trade. The impending encounter was likely to be as sweet for Don Francisco as it would certainly be bitter for Captain Blood. Even in prosperity Don Francisco would not have been likely to spare him. In adversity, the prospect of earning fifty thousand pieces of eight would serve to sharpen the vindictiveness of this official who had fallen upon evil days.

Shuddering at the narrowness of the escape, thankful for that timeliest of warnings, Captain Blood perceived that there was only one thing to be done. Impossible now to await the coming of the Dutchman in the morning. In some sort of vessel, alone, if need be in an open boat, he must get out of Rio de La Hacha at once. But he must not appear either startled or in flight.

He frowned annoyance. 'What misfortune that I should have been absent when Don Francisco called. It is intolerable to put a gentleman born to the trouble of seeking me again. I will wait upon him at once, if you will tell me where he is lodged.'

'Oh, certainly. You will find his house in the Calle San Blas; that is the first turning on your right; anyone there will show you where Don Francisco lives.'

The Captain waited for no more.

'I go at once,' he said, and stepped out.

But either he forgot, or he mistook the landlord's directions, for, instead of turning to his right, he turned to his left and took his way briskly down a street, at this hour of supper almost deserted, that led towards the harbour.

He was passing an alley, within fifty yards of the mole, when from the depths of it came ominous sounds of strife; the clash of steel on steel, a woman's cry, and a man's harsh, vituperative interjections.

The concern supplied him by his own situation might well have reminded him that these murderous sounds were no affair of his, and that he had enough already on his hands to get out of Rio de La Hacha with his life. But the actual message of the vituperative exclamation overheard, arrested his flight.

'*Perro inglés!* Dog of an Englishman!'

Thus Blood learnt that in that dark alley it was a compatriot who was being murdered. It was enough. In foreign lands, to any man who is not dead to feeling, a compatriot is a brother. He plunged at once into the gloom of that narrow way, his hand groping for the pistol inside the breast of his coat.

As he ran, however, it occurred to him that here was noise enough already. The last thing he desired was to attract spectators by increasing it. So he left the pistol in his pocket and whipped out his rapier instead.

By the little light that lingered, he could make out the group as he advanced upon it. Three men were assailing a fourth, who, with his back to a closed door and his left arm swathed in his coat so as to make a buckler, offered a defence that was as desperate as it must ultimately prove futile. That he could have stood so long even against such odds was evidence of an unusual toughness.

At a little distance beyond that brawling quartet, the slight figure of a woman, cloaked and hooded by a light mantle of black silk, leaned in helplessness against the wall.

Blood's intervention was stealthy, swift, and practical. He announced his arrival by sending his sword through the back of the nearest of the three assailants.

'That will adjust the odds,' he explained, and cleared

his blade just in time to engage a gentleman who whirled
to face him, spitting blasphemies with that fluency in
which the Castilian has no equal.

Blood broke ground nimbly, enveloped the vicious
thrust in a counter-parry, and in the movement drove
his steel through the blasphemer's sword-arm.

Out of action, the man reeled back, gripping the arm
from which the blood was spurting and cursing more
fluently than ever, whilst the only remaining Spaniard,
perceiving the sudden change in the odds, from three
to one on his side to two to one against it, and not
relishing this at all, gave way before Blood's charge. In
the next moment he and his wounded comrade were in
flight, leaving their friend to lie where he had fallen.

At Blood's side the man he had rescued, breathing
in gasps, almost collapsed against him.

'Damned assassins!' he panted. 'Another minute
would ha' seen the end of me.'

Then the woman who had darted forward surged at
his other side.

'*Vamos, Jorgito! Vamos!*' she cried in fearful urgency. Then shifted from Spanish to fairly fluent English. 'Quick, my love! Let us get to the boat. We are
almost there. Oh, come!'

This mention of a boat was an intimation to Blood
that his good action was not likely to go unrewarded. It
gave him every ground for hoping that, in helping a
stranger, he had helped himself; for a boat was, of all
things, what he most needed at the moment.

His hands played briskly over the man he was supporting, and came away wet from his left shoulder. He
made no more ado. He hitched the fellow's right arm
around his neck, gripped him about the waist to support
him and bade the girl lead on.

Whatever her panic on the score of her man's hurt,
the promptitude of her obedience to the immediate need
of getting him away was in itself an evidence of her
courage and practical wit. One or two windows in the
alley had been thrust open, and from odd doorways
white faces dimly seen in the gloom were peering out to

discover the cause of the hubbub. These watchers, though silent, and perhaps timid, stressed the need for haste.

'Come,' she said. 'This way. Follow me.'

Half-supporting, half-carrying the wounded man, Blood kept pace with her speed, and so came out of the alley and gained the mole. Across this, disregarding the stare of odd wayfarers who paused and turned as they went by, she led him to a spot where a longboat waited.

Two men rose out of it: Indians, or half-castes, their bodies naked from shoulder to waist. One of them sprang instantly ashore, then checked peering in the dusk at the man Captain Blood was supporting.

'*Que tal el patrón?*' he asked gruffly.

'He has been hurt. Help him down carefully. Oh, make haste! Make haste!'

She remained on the quay, casting fearful glances over her shoulder whilst Blood and the Indians were bestowing the wounded man in the sternsheets. Then Blood, standing in the boat, proffered her his hand.

'Aboard, ma'am.' He was peremptory, and so as to save time and argument, he added: 'I am coming with you.'

'But you can't! We sail at once. The boat will not return. We dare not linger, sir.'

'Faith, no more dare I. It is very well. I've said I am coming with you. Aboard, ma'am!' and without more ado, he almost pulled her into the boat, ordering the men to give way.

2

If she found the matter bewildering, she did not pursue it. Concern enough for her at the moment lay in the condition of her Englishman and the evidently urgent need of getting him away before his assailants returned, reinforced, to finish him. She could not waste moments so precious in arguing with an eccentric: possibly she had not even any thoughts to spare him.

As the boat shot away from the mole, she sank down in the sternsheets at the side of her companion, who had swooned. On his other side, Blood was kneeling, and the deft fingers of the buccaneer who once had been a surgeon located and gropingly examined that wound, high in the shoulder.

'Give yourself peace,' he comforted the girl. 'This is no great matter. A little blood-letting has made him faint. That is all. You'll soon have him well again.'

She breathed a little prayer of thanks. *'Gracias a Dios!'*

Then, with a backward glance in the direction of the mole, urged the men to greater effort.

As the boat sped over the dark water towards a ship's lantern a half-mile away, the Englishman stirred and looked about him.

'What the plague . . .' he began, and struggled to rise.

Blood's hands restrained him.

'Quiet,' he said. 'There's no need for alarm. We're taking you aboard.'

'Taking me aboard? Who the devil are you?'

'Jorgito,' the girl cried, 'it is the gentleman who saved your life.'

'Odso! You're there, Isabelita?' His next question showed that he took in the situation. 'Are they following?'

When she had reassured him and pointed ahead to the ship's lantern towards which they were heading, he laughed softly, then cursed the Indians.

'Faster, you lazy dogs! Bend your backs to it, you louts!'

The rowers increased their effort, breathing stertorously. The man laughed again, softly as before, a fleering, mocking sound.

'So, so. We've had the luck to win clear of that gin, with no more than a scratch. Yet, God's my life, it's more than a scratch. I'm bleeding like a Christian martyr.'

'It's nothing,' Blood reassured him. 'You've lost

some blood. But once aboard we'll staunch the wound
and make you comfortable.'

'Faith, you talk like a sawbones.'

'It's what I am.'

'Gadso! Was there ever greater luck! Eh, Isabelita?
A swordsman to rescue me and a doctor to head me, all
in one. There's Providence watching over me this night.
An omen, sweetheart.'

'A mercy,' she corrected on a crooning note, and
drew closer to him.

And now, from their scraps of talk, Blood pieced together the tale of their exact relationship. They were
an eloping pair, these two, this Englishman, whose name
was George Fairfax, and this little *hidalga* of the great
family of Sotomayor. His late assailants were her brother and two friends, bent upon frustrating the elopement.
Her brother was the Spaniard who had escaped un-
injured from the encounter, and it was his pursuit in
force which she dreaded and for which she continually
looked back towards the receding mole. By the time,
however, that agitated lights came dancing at last along
the water's edge, the longboat was in the black shadow
of a two-masted brig, bumping against her side, whilst
from her deck a gruff English voice was hailing them.

The lady was the first to swarm the accommodation-
ladder. Then followed Fairfax, with Blood immediately
and so closely behind as to support him and, indeed,
partly carry him aboard.

At the head of the ladder they were received by a
large man with a face that showed hot in the light of a
lantern slung from the mainmast, who overwhelmed
them with alarmed questions.

Fairfax, steadying himself against the bulkhead,
gasped for breath, and broke into that interrogatory flow
sharply to rap out his orders.

'Get under way, at once, Tim! No time to get the
boat aboard. Take her in tow. And don't stay to take
up anchor. Cut the cable. Hoist sail and let's away.
Thank God the wind serves. We shall have the Alcalde

and all the *alguaziles* of La Hacha aboard if we delay.
So stir your damned bones.'

Tim's roaring voice was passing on the orders and
men were leaping to obey when the lady set a hand on
her lover's arm.

'But this gentleman, George. You forget him. He does
not know where we go.'

Fairfax supported himself with a hand on Blood's
shoulder. He turned his head to peer into the countenance of his preserver, and there was a scowl on the
lean, dark face.

'Ye'll have gathered I can't be delayed,' he said.

'Faith, it's very glad to gather it I've been,' was the
easy answer. 'And it's little I'm caring where you go, so
long as it's away from Rio de La Hacha.'

The dark face lightened. The man laughed softly.

'Running away, too, are you? Damn my blood!
You're most accommodating. It seems all of a piece.
Look alive, Tim! Can these lubbers of yours move no
faster?'

There was a blast from the master's whistle and naked
feet pattered at speed across the deck. Tim spoke briskly
and savagely, to stimulate their efforts, then sprang to
the side to shout his orders to the Indians still in the
boat alongside.

'Get you below, sir,' he begged his employer. 'I'll
come to you as soon as we are under way and the
course is set.'

It was Blood who assisted Fairfax to the cabin, a
place of fair proportions, if rudely equipped, lighted by
a slush-lamp that swung above the bare table. The lady,
breathing tenderest solicitude, followed closely.

To receive them a Negro lad emerged from a stateroom on the larboard side. He cried out at sight of the
blood with which his master's shirt was drenched, and
stood arrested, teeth and eyeballs flashing in that startled, dusky face.

Assuming authority, Blood ordered the Negro to lend
a hand, and between them they carried Fairfax, whose
senses were beginning to swim again, through the door-

way which the steward had left open, and there removed his shoes and got him to bed.

Then Blood despatched the boy, who answered to the name of Alcatrace, to the galley for hot water and to the captain for the ship's medicine chest.

On the narrow bed Fairfax, a man as tall and well-knit as Blood himself, reclined in a sitting posture, propped by all the pillows available. He wore his own hair, and the reddish-brown cloud of it half-veiled his pallid, bony countenance as with eyes half-closed his head lolled weakly forward.

Having disposed him comfortably, Blood cut away his sodden shirt and laid bare his vigorous torso.

When the steward returned with a can of water, some linen, and a cedax box containing the ship's poor store of medicines, the lady followed him into the stateroom, begging to be allowed to help. Through the ports that stood open to the purple, tropical night, she had heard the creak of blocks and the thud of the sails as they took the wind, and it was with immense relief that she felt at last under her feet the forward heave of the un-leashed brig. One anxiety at least was now allayed and the danger of recapture overpast.

Courteously Blood welcomed her assistance. Observing her now in the light, he found her to agree with the impressions he had already formed. A slight wisp of womanhood, little more than a child, and probably not long out of the hands of the nuns, she showed him a winsome, eager face, and two shining eyes intensely black against the waxen pallor in which they were set. Her gold-laced gown of black, with beautiful point of Spain at throat and wrists, and some pearls of obvious price entwined in her glossy tresses, were, like the proud air investing her, those of a person of rank.

She proved quick to understand Blood's requirements and deft to execute them, and thus, with her assistance, he worked upon the man for love of whom this little *hidalga* of the great house of Sotomayor was apparently burning her boats. Carefully, tenderly, he washed the purple lips of the wound in the shoulder, which was still oozing. In the medicine chest held for him by Alcatrace, he discovered at least some arnica, and of this he made a liberal application. It produced a fiercely reviving effect. Fairfax threw up his head.

'Hell-fire!' he cried. 'Do you burn me, damn you?'

'Patience, sir. Patience. It's a healing cautery.'

The lady's arm encircled the patient's head, supporting and soothing him. Her lips lightly touched his dank brow. 'My poor Jorgito,' she murmured.

He grunted for answer, and closed his eyes.

Blood was tearing linen into strips. Out of these he made a pad for the wound, applied a bandage to hold it in position, and then a second bandage, like a sling, to keep the left arm immovable against the patient's breast. Then Alcatrace found him a fresh shirt, and they passed it over the Englishman's head, leaving the left sleeve empty. The surgical task was finished.

Blood made a readjustment of the pillows.

'Ye'll sleep in that position, if you please. And you'll avoid movement as much as possible. If we can keep you quiet, you should be whole again in a week at most. Ye've had a near escape. Had the blade taken you two inches lower, it's another kind of bed we'ld be making for you this minute. Ye've been lucky, so you have.'

'Lucky? May I burn!'

'There's even, perhaps, something for which to render thanks.'

If the quiet reminder brought from Fairfax no more than a grumbled oath, it stirred the lady to a sort of violence. She leaned across the narrow bed to seize both of Blood's hands. Her pale, dark face was solemnly intense. Her lips trembled, as did her voice.

'You have been so good, so brave, so noble.'

Before he could guess her intent, she had carried his hands to her lips and kissed them. Protesting, he wrenched them away. She smiled up at him wistfully.

'But shall I not kiss them, then, those hands? Have they not save' my Jorgito's life? Have they not heal' his

wounds? All my life I shall love those hands. All my life
I shall be grateful to them.'

Captain Blood had his doubts about this. He was not
finding Jorgito prepossessing. The fellow's shallow, slop-
ing, animal brow and wide, loose-lipped mouth inspired
no confidence, for all that in its total sum, and in a
coarse raffish way, the face might be described as handsome. It was a face of strongly marked bone structures,
the nose boldly carved, the cheek-bones prominent, the
jaw long and powerful. In age, he could not have passed
the middle thirties.

His eyes, rather close-set and pale, shifted under
Blood's scrutiny, and he began to mutter belated ac-
knowledgments, reminded by the lady's outburst of
what was due from him.

'I vow sir, I am deeply in your debt. Damn my blood!
That's nothing new for me, God knows. I've been in
somebody's debt ever since I can remember. But this
—may I perish!—is a debt of another kind. If only you
had skewered for me the guts of that pimp who got
away, I'd be still more grateful to you. The world could
very well do without Don Serafino de Sotomayor. Damn
his blood!'

'*Señor Jesús! No digas eso, querido!*' Quick and shrill
came the remonstrance from the little *hidalga*. 'Don't
say such things, my love.' To soften her protest, she
stroked his cheek as she ran on. 'No, no, Jorgito. If that
have happen, never more will my conscience be quiet.
If my brother's blood have been shed, it will kill me.'

'And what of my blood, then? Hasn't there been
enough of that shed by him and his plaguey bullies?
And didn't he hope to shed it all, the damned cut-
throat?'

'*Querido,*' she soothed him. 'That was for protect me.
He think it his duty. I could not have forgive' him ever
if he kill you. It would have broke my heart, Jorgito,
you know. Yet, I can understand Serafino. Oh, let us
thank God—God and this so brave gentleman—that no
worse have happen'.'

And then Tim, the big red shipmaster, rolled in to

inquire how Mr. Fairfax fared, and to report that the
course was set, that the *Heron* was moving briskly before a steady southerly breeze, and that already La
Hacha was half-a-dozen miles astern. 'So all's well that
ends well, sir. And we've to find quarters for this gentleman who came aboard with you. I'll have a hammock
slung for him in the cuddy. See to it, Alcatrace.' He
drove the Negro out upon that task. *'Pronto! Vamos!'*

Fairfax reclined with half-closed eyes. 'All's well that
ends well,' he echoed.

He laughed softly, and Blood observed that always,
when he laughed, his loose mouth seemed to writhe in a
sneer. He was recovering vigour of body and of mind
with every moment now, since he had been made comfortable and the bleeding had been checked. His hand
closed over the lady's where it lay upon the counter-
pane.

'Ay. All's well that ends well,' he repeated. 'Ye'll
have the jewels safe, sweetheart?'

'The jewels?' She started, caught her breath, and for
a moment her brows were knit in thought. Then, with
consternation overspreading her countenance and a
hand on her heart, she came to her feet. 'The jewels!'

Fairfax slewed his head round to look at her fully,
his pale eyes suddenly wide, the brows raised.

'What now?' His voice was a croak. 'Ye have them
safe?'

Her lip quivered. *'Valga me Dios!* I must have drop'
the casket when Serafino overtake us.'

There was a long, hushed pause, which Blood felt to
be of the kind that is the prelude of a storm.

'Ye dropped the casket!' said Fairfax. His tone was
ominously quiet. He was staring at her in stupefaction,
his jaw loose. 'Ye dropped the casket?' Gradually a
blaze kindled in his light eyes. 'D'ye say ye dropped the
casket?' This time his voice rose and cracked. 'Damn my
blood! It passes belief! Hell! Ye can't have dropped it.'

The sudden fury of him shocked her. She looked at
him with frightened eyes.

'You are angry, Jorgito,' she faltered. 'But you must

not be angry. That is not right. Think of what happen'. I was distracted. Your life was in danger. What were jewels then? How can I think of jewels? I let the casket fall. I did not notice. Then, when you are wounded, and I think perhaps you will die, can I think of jewels then? You see, Jorgito? It is *lastima*, yes. But they do not matter. We have each other. They do not matter. Let them go.'

Her fond hand was stealing about his neck again. But in a rage, he flung it off.

'Don't matter!' he roared, his loose mouth working. 'Rot my bones! You lose a fortune; you spill thirty thousand ducats in the kennel, and you say it don't matter! Hell and the Devil, girl! If that don't matter, tell me what does.'

Blood thought it time to intervene. Gently, but very firmly, he pressed the wounded man back upon his pillows.

'Will you be quiet now, ye bellowing calf? Haven't you spilt enough of your blood this night?'

But Fairfax raged and struggled.

'Quiet? Damn my soul! You don't understand. How can I be quiet? Quiet, when this little fool has . . .'

She interrupted him there. She had drawn herself stiffly erect. Her lips were steady now, her eyes more intensely black than ever.

'Is it so much to you that I lose my jewels, George? They were my jewels. You'll please to remember that. If I lose them, I lose them, and it is my affair; my loss. And I should not count it loss in a night when I have gain' so much. Or have I not, George? Were the jewels such great matter to you? More than I, perhaps?'

That challenge brought him to his senses. He beat a retreat before it, in the best order he could contrive, paused, and then broke into a laugh that to Blood was pure play-acting.

'What the devil! Are you angry with me, Isabelita? Plague on it! I am like that. Hot and quick. That's my nature. And thirty thousand ducats is a loss to make a man forget his manners for the moment. But the jewels?

Bah! Rot the jewels! If they've gone, they've gone.' He held out a coaxing hand. 'Come, Isabelita. Kiss and forgive, sweetheart. I'll soon be buying you all the jewels you could want.'

'I want no jewels, George.' She was not more than half-mollified. Something of the ugly suspicion he had aroused in her still lingered. But she went to him, and suffered him to put an arm about her. 'You must not be angry with me again, ever, Jorgito. If I had love' you less, I would have think more of the casket.'

'To be sure you would, chick. To be sure.'

Tim shuffled uncomfortably.

'I'ld best get back on deck, sir.' He made shift to go. But in the doorway, paused to turn to Captain Blood. 'That blackamoor will ha' slung your hammock, for you.'

'You may be showing me the way, then. There's no more I can do here for tonight.'

Whilst the shipmaster waited, holding the door, he spoke again. 'If this wind holds, we should make Port Royal by Sunday night or Monday morning.'

Blood was brought to a standstill.

'Port Royal?' said he slowly. 'I'ld not care to land there.'

Fairfax looked at him.

'Why not? It's an English settlement. You should have nothing to fear in Jamaica.'

'Still I'ld not care to land there. What port will you be making after that?'

The question seemed to amuse Fairfax. Again he uttered his unpleasant, fleering laugh.

'Faith, that'll depend upon a mort o' things.'

Blood's steadily rising dislike of the man sharpened his rejoinder.

'I'ld thank you to make it depend a little upon my convenience, seeing that I'm here for yours.'

'For mine?' Fairfax raised his light brows. 'Od rot me, now! Didn't I understand you was running away, too? But we'll see what we can do. Where was you wishing to be put ashore?'

By an effort Blood stifled his indignation and kept to the point.

'From Port Royal it would be no great matter for you to carry me through the Windward Passage, and land me either on the northwest coast of Hispaniola or even on Tortuga.'

'Tortuga!' There was such a quickening of the light, shifty eyes that Blood instantly regretted that he should have mentioned the place. Fairfax was pondering him intently, and behind that searching glance it was obvious that his mind was busy. 'Tortuga, eh? So ye've friends among the buccaneers?' He laughed. 'Well, well! That's your affair, to be sure. Let the *Heron* make Port Royal first, and then we'll be obliging you.'

'I'll be in your debt,' said Blood, with more than a hint of sarcasm. 'Give you good-night, sir. And you, ma'am.'

3

For a considerable time after the door had closed upon the departing men, Fairfax lay very still and very thoughtful, his eyes narrowed, a mysterious smile on his lips.

At long last, Doña Isabel spoke softly.

'You should sleep, Jorgito. Of what are you thinking?'

He made her an answer that seemed to hold no sense.

'Of the difference the lack of a periwig makes to a man who's an Irishman and a surgeon and wants to be landed on Tortuga.'

For a moment she wondered whether he had a touch of fever, and it increased her concern that he should sleep. She proposed to leave him. But he would not hear of it. He cursed the burning thirst he discovered in himself, and begged her to give him to drink. That same thirst continued thereafter to torment him and to keep him wakeful, so that she stayed at his side and gave him frequent draughts of water, mixed with the juice of limes, and once, on his insistent demand, with brandy.

The night wore on, with little said between them, and after some three hours of it he turned so quiet that she thought he slept at last and was preparing to creep away when suddenly he announced his complete wakefulness by an oath and a laugh and ordered her to summon Tim. She obeyed only because to demur would be to excite him.

When Tim returned with her, Fairfax required to know what o'clock it might be and how far the master reckoned they had travelled. Eight bells, said Tim, had just been made, and they had put already a good fifty miles between the *Heron* and La Hacha.

Then came a question that was entirely odd: 'How far to Cartagena?'

'A hundred miles, maybe. Maybe a trifle more.'

'How long to make it?'

The shipmaster's eyes became round with surprise.

'With the wind as it blows, maybe twenty-four hours.'

'Make it, then,' was the astounding order. 'Go about at once.'

The surprise in Tim's hot face was changed to concern.

'Ye've the fever, Captain, surely. What should we be doing back on the Main?'

'I've no fever, man. Ye've heard my order. Go about and lay a course for Cartagena.'

'But Cartagena . . .' The mate and Doña Isabel exchanged glances.

Surprising this, and perceiving what was in their minds, Fairfax's mouth twisted ill-humouredly.

'Od rot you! Wait!' he growled and fell to thinking.

Had he been in full possession of his vigour, he would have admitted no partner to the evil enterprise he had in mind. He would have carried it through single-handed, keeping his own counsel. But his condition making him dependent upon the master left him no choice, as he saw it, but to lay his cards upon the table.

'Riconete is at Cartagena, and Riconete will pay fifty

thousand pieces of eight for Captain Blood, dead or alive. Fifty thousand pieces of eight.' He paused a moment, and then added: 'That's a mort o' money, and there'll be five thousand pieces for you, Tim, when it's paid.'

Tim's suspicions were now a certainty. 'To be sure. To be sure.'

Exasperated, Fairfax snarled at him. 'God rot your bones, Tim, are you humouring me? Ye think I have the fever. Ye'ld be the better yourself for a touch of the fever that's burning me. It might sharpen your paltry wits and quicken your sight.'

'Ay, ay,' said Tim. 'But where do we find Captain Blood?'

'In the cuddy, where you've bestowed him.'

'Ye're light-headed, Captain.'

'Will you harp on that? Damn you for a fool! That is Captain Blood, I tell you. I recognized him the moment he asked to be landed at Tortuga. I'ld ha' known him sooner if I'ld ha' been more than half-awake. He wouldn't care to land at Port Royal, he said. Of course he wouldn't. Not while Colonel Bishop is Governor of Jamaica. That'll maybe help you to understand.'

Tim was foolishly blinking his amazement and loosed an oath or two of surprised conviction.

'Ye recognize him, d'ye say?'

'That's what I say, and ye may believe I'm not mistook. Be off now, and put about. That first. Then you'ld better see to making this fellow fast. If you take him in his sleep, it'll save trouble. Away with you.'

'Ay, ay,' said Tim, and bustled off in a state of excitement that was tempered by no scruples.

Doña Isabel, in a horror that had been growing steadily with understanding of what she heard, came suddenly to her feet.

'Wait, wait! What is it you will do?'

'No matter for you, sweetheart,' said Fairfax, and a peremptory wave of his sound hand dismissed Tim from the doorway where her voice had arrested him.

'But it is matter for me. I understand. You cannot do this, George.'

'Can't I? Why, the rogue'll be asleep by now. It should be easy. There'll be a surprised awakening for him; there will so.' And his hearty laugh went to increase her horror.

'But—*Dios mio!*—you cannot, you cannot. You cannot sell the man who save' your life.'

He turned his head to consider her with sneering amusement. Too much of a scoundrel to know how much of a scoundrel he was, he imagined himself opposed by a foolish, sentimental qualm that would be easily allayed. He was confident, too, of his complete ascendancy over a mind whose innocence he mistook for simplicity.

'Rot me, child, it's a duty, no less. You don't understand. This Blood is a pirate rogue, buccaneer, thief, and assassin. The sea'll be cleaner without him.'

She only became more vehement.

'He may be what you say; pirate, buccaneer, and the rest. Of that, I know nothing. I care nothing. But I know he save' your life, and I care for that. He is here in your ship because he save' your life.'

'That's a lie, anyway,' growled Fairfax. 'He's here because he's took advantage of my condition. He's come aboard the *Heron* so as to escape from the Main and the justice that is after him. Well, well. He'll find out his mistake tomorrow.'

She wrung her hands, a fierce distress in her white face. Then, growing steadier, she pondered him very solemnly with an expression he had never yet seen on that eager face, an expression that annoyed him.

The faith in this man, of whom, after all, she knew but little, the illusions formed about him in the course of being swept off her maiden feet by a whirlwind wooing, which had made her cast everything away so that at his bidding she might link her fortunes with his own, had been sorely disturbed by the spectacle of his coarse anger at the loss of the jewels. That faith was now in danger of being finally and tragically shattered

by this revelation of a nature which must fill her with
dread and loathing once she admitted to herself the
truth of what she beheld. Against this admission she
was still piteously struggling. For if George Fairfax
should prove, indeed, the thing she was being compelled
to suspect, what could there be for her who was now
so completely and irrevocably in his power?

'George,' she said quietly, in a forced calm to which
the tumult of her bosom gave the lie, 'it not matters
what this man is. You owe him your life. Without him,
you would lie dead now in that alley in La Hacha. You
cannot do what you say. It would be infamy.'

'Infamy? Infamy be damned!' He laughed his ugly,
contemptuous laugh. 'Ye just don't understand. It's duty
I tell you. The duty of every honest gentleman to lay
this pirate rogue by the heels.'

Scorn deepened in the dark eyes that continued so
disconcertingly to regard him.

'Honest? You say that! Honest to sell the man who
save' your life? For fifty thousand pieces of eight, was
it not? That is honest? Honest as Judas, who sell the
Saviour for thirty pieces.'

He glowered at her in resentment. Then found, as
rogues will, an argument to justify himself.

'If you don't like it, you may blame yourself. If in
your stupidity you hadn't lost the jewels, I shouldn't
need to do this. As it is, it's just a Providence. For how
else am I to pay Tim and the hands, buy stores at Jamaica, and pay for the graving of the *Heron* against the
ocean voyage? How else?'

'How else!' There was a bitter edge to her voice now.
'How else since I lose my jewels, eh? It is so. It was for
that? My jewels were for that? *Que verguenza!*' A sob
shook her. '*Dios mio, que viltad! Ay de mi! Ay de mi!*'

Then, hoping against hope in her despair, she caught
his arm in her two hands and changed her tone to one
of pleading. 'Jorgito . . .'

But Mr. Fairfax, you'll have gathered, was not a
patient man. He would be plagued no further. He flung

her off with a violence that sent her hurtling against the bulkhead at her back. His evil temper was now thoroughly aroused, and it may have been rendered the more savage because his impetuous movement brought a twinge of pain to his wounded shoulder.

'Enough of that whining, my girl. Devil take you if you haven't set me bleeding again. Ye'll meddle in things you understand and not in my affairs. D'ye think a man's to be pestered so? Ye'll have to learn different afore we're acquainted much longer. Ye will so, by God!' Peremptorily he ended: 'Get you to bed.'

As she still lingered, winded where he had flung her, white-faced, aghast, incredulous, annoying him by the reproach of her stare, he raised his voice in fury.

'D'ye hear me? Get you to bed, rot you! Go!'

She went without another word, so swiftly and quietly that she left him with a sense of something ominous. Uneasy, a sudden suspicion of treachery crossing his mind, he got gingerly down from his bed despite his condition, and staggered to the door, to spy upon her thence. He was just in time to see her vanish through the doorway of the stateroom opposite, and a moment later, from beyond her closed door, a sound of desolate sobbing reached him across the cabin.

His upper lip curled as he listened. At least, it had not occurred to her to betray his intentions to Captain Blood. Not that it would matter much if she did. Tim and the six hands aboard would easily account for the buccaneer if he should make trouble. Still, the notion might come to her, and it would be safer to provide.

He bawled the name of Alcatrace, who lay stretched, asleep, on the stern locker. The steward, awakened by the call, leapt up to answer it, and received from Fairfax stern, clear orders to remain awake and on guard so as to see that Doña Isabel did not leave the cabin. At need, he was to employ violence to prevent it.

Then, with the help of Alcatrace, Fairfax crawled back to his bed, resettled himself, and soon, a heavy list to starboard informing him that they had gone about, this man, who accounted his fortune made, allowed himself to sink at last into an exhausted sleep.

4

It should have occurred to them that the list to starboard, so reassuring to Mr. George Fairfax, must present a riddle to Captain Blood if he should happen still to be awake. And awake it happened that he was.

He had doffed no more than his coat and his shoes, and he lay in shirt and breeches in the hammock they had slung for him in the stuffy, narrow spaces of the cuddy, vainly wooing a slumber that held aloof. He was preoccupied, and not at all on his own behalf. Not all the rude ways that he had followed and the disillusions that he had suffered had yet sufficed to extinguish the man's sentimental nature. In the case of the little lady of the house of Sotomayor, he found abundant if disturbing entertainment for it this night. He was perplexed and perturbed by the situation in which he discovered her, so utterly in the power of a man who was not merely and unmistakeably a scoundrel, but a crude egotist of little mind and less heart. Captain Blood reflected upon the misery and heart-break that so often will follow upon an innocent girl's infatuation for just such a man, who has obtained empire over her by his obvious but flashy vigour and the deceptive ardour of his wooing. In the buccaneer's sentimental eyes, she was as a dove in the talons of a hawk, and he would give a deal to deliver her from them before she was torn to pieces. But it was odds that in her infatuation, she would not welcome that deliverance, and even if, proving an exception to the rule, she should lend an ear to the sense that Blood could talk to her, he realized that he was in no case to offer her assistance, however ardently he might desire to do so.

With a sigh he sought to dismiss a problem to which he could supply no happy solution; but it persisted until that list to starboard of a ship that hitherto had ridden on an even keel came to divert his attention into other channels. Was it possible, he wondered, that the wind could have veered with such suddenness? It must be so, because nothing else would explain the fact observed; at least, nothing else that seemed reasonable.

Nevertheless, he was moved to ascertain. He eased himself out of the hammock, groped for his coat and his shoes, put them on, and made his way by the gangway to the ship's waist.

Here one of the hands squatted on the hatch-coaming, softly singing, and at the break of the low poop the helmsman stood at the whipstaff. But Blood asked no questions of either of them. He preferred instead to obtain from the heavens the information that he sought, and the clear, starry sky told him all that he required to know. The North Star was abeam on the starboard quarter. Thus he obtained the surprising knowledge that they had gone about.

Always prudently mistrustful of anything that appeared to be against reason, he climbed the poop in quest of Tim. He beheld him pacing there, a burly silhouette against the light from the two tall stern lanterns, and he stepped briskly towards him.

To the shipmaster Captain Blood's advent was momentarily disconcerting. At that very instant he had been asking himself whether sufficient time had been given their passenger to be fast asleep, so that they might tie him up in his hammock without unnecessary ado. Recovering from his surprise, Tim jovially hailed the Captain as he advanced across the canting deck.

'A fine night, sir.'

Blood took a devious way to his ends, by an answer that applied a test.

'I see the wind has changed.'

'Ay,' the mate answered, with alacrity. 'It was uncommon sudden. It's come to blow hard from the south.'

'That'll be delaying us in making Port Royal.'

'If it holds. But maybe it'll change again.'

'Maybe it will,' said Blood. 'We'll pray for it.'

Pacing together, they had come to the rail. They leaned upon it, and looked down at the dark water and the white, luminous edge of the wave that curled away from the ship's flank.

Blood made philosophy.

'A queer, uncertain life, this seafaring life, Tim, at the mercy of every wind that blows, driving us now in one direction, now in another, sometimes helping, sometimes hindering, and sometimes defeating and destroying us. I suppose you love your life, Tim?'

'What a question! To be sure, I love my life.'

'And ye'll have the fear of death that's common to us all?'

'Od rot me! Ye're talking like a parson.'

'Maybe. Ye see it's opportune to remind you that ye're mortal, Tim. We're all apt to forget it at times and place ourself in dangers that are entirely unnecessary. Mortal dangers. Just such a danger as you stand in this very minute, Tim.'

'What's that?' Tim took his elbows from the rail.

'Now don't be moving,' said Blood gently. His hand was inside the breast of his coat, and from the region of it, under cover of the cloth, something hard and tubular was pressed closely into the mate's side just below the ribs. 'My finger's on the trigger, Tim, and if ye were to move suddenly, ye might startle me into pulling it. Put your elbows back on the rail, Tim darling, while we talk. Ye've nothing to fear. I've no notion of hurting you; that is, provided ye're reasonable, as I think ye will be. Tell me now: Why are we going back to the Main?'

Tim was gasping in mingled surprise and fear, and his fear was greater, perhaps, than it need have been because he knew now beyond doubt with whom he had to deal. The sweat stood in cold beads on his brow.

'Going back to the Main?' he faltered stupidly.

'Just so. Why have ye gone about? And why did ye lie to me about a south wind? D'ye think I'm such a lubber that I can't tell north from south on a clear night like this? Ye're no better than a fool, it seems. But unless ye get sense enough not to lie to me again, ye'll never tell another lie to anyone after this night. Now I'll be asking you again: Why are we going back to the Main? And don't tell me it's Fairfax you're selling.'

There was on Tim's part a thoughtful, hard-breathing pause. Blood might have made him afraid to lie, but he was still more afraid to speak the truth, since it was what it was.

'Who else should it be?' he growled.

'Tim, Tim! Ye're lying to me again despite my warning. And your lies have the queer quality of telling me the truth. For if ye were meaning to sell Fairfax, it's La Hacha ye'ld be making for; and if ye were making for La Hacha ye'ld never be reaching so far on this westerly tack unless ye're a lubberly idiot, which I perceive ye're not. I'm saving you the trouble of lying again, Tim, for that—I vow to God—would certainly be the death of you. D'ye know who I am? Let me have the truth of that, too. Do you?'

It was just because he did know who his questioner was that, having twice been so easily caught out in falsehood by this man's acuteness, the mate stood chilled and palsied, never doubting that if he moved his inside would be blown out by that pistol in his flank. Fear, at last, tore the truth from him.

'I do, Captain. But . . .'

'Whisht now! Don't be committing suicide by telling me another falsehood; and there's no need. There's no need to tell me more. I know the rest. Ye're heading for Cartagena, of course. That's the market for the goods you carry, and the Marquis of Riconete is your buyer. If the notion is yours, Tim, I can forgive it. For you owe me nothing, and there's no reason in the world why ye shouldn't be earning fifty thousand pieces of eight by selling me to Spain. Is the notion yours, now?'

Vehemently Tim invoked the heavenly hierarchy to bear witness that he had done no more than obey the orders of Fairfax, who alone had conceived this infamous notion of making for Cartagena. He was still protesting when Blood cut into that flow of blasphemy-reinforced assertion.

'Yes, yes. I believe you. I had a notion that he recognized me when I spoke of landing on Tortuga. It was incautious of me. But—bad cess to him!—I'd saved his mangy life, and I thought that even the worst blackguard in the Caribbean would hesitate before . . . No matter. Tell me this: What share were you to have of the blood money, Tim?'

'Five thousand pieces, he promised,' said Tim, hangdog.

'Glory be! Is that all? Ye can't be much of a hand at a bargain; and that's not the only kind of fool you are. How long did you think you'ld live to enjoy the money? Or perhaps you didn't think. Well, think now, Tim, and maybe it'll occur to you that when it was known, as known it would be, how ye'd earned it, my buccaneers would hunt you to the ends of the seas. Ye should reflect on these things, Tim, when ye go partners with a scoundrel. Ye'll be wiser to throw in your lot with me, my lad. And if it's five thousand pieces you want, faith, you may still earn them by taking my orders whilst I'm aboard this brig. Do that, and you may call for the money at Tortuga when you please, and be sure of safe-conduct. You have my word for that. And I am Captain Blood.'

Tim required no time for reflection. From the black shadow of imminent death that had been upon him, he saw himself suddenly not only offered safety, but a reward as great as that which villainy would have brought him, and free from those overlooked risks to which Blood had just drawn his attention.

'I take the Almighty to be my witness . . .' he was beginning with fervour, when again Blood cut him short.

'Now don't be wasting breath on oaths; for I put no trust in them. My trust is in the gold I offer on the one hand and the lead on the other. I'm not leaving your side from this moment, Tim. I've conceived a kindness for you, my lad. And if I take my pistol from your ribs, don't be presuming upon that. It stays primed and cocked. Ye've no pistols of your own about you, I hope.' He ran his left hand over the mate's body, as he spoke, so as to assure himself. 'Very well. We'll not go about again as you might be supposing, because we are still going back to the Main. But not to Cartagena. It's for La Hacha that we'll be steering a course. So you'll just be stepping to the poop-rail with me, and bidding them put the helm over. Ye've run far enough westward. It's more than time we were on the other tack if we are to make La Hacha by morning. Come along now.'

Obediently the master went with him, and from the rail piped the hands to quarters. When all was ready, his deep voice rang out.

'Let go, and haul!' and a moment later, in response, the foreyards ran round noisily, the deck came level and then canted to larboard, and the brig was heading southeast.

5

All through that clear June night Captain Blood and the master of the *Heron* remained side by side on the poop of the brig, whether sitting or standing or going ever and anon to the rail to issue orders to the crew. And though the voice was always Tim's, the orders were always Captain Blood's.

Tim gave him no trouble, it never being in his mind to change a state of things which suited his rascality so well. The reckoning there might have to be with Fairfax gave him no concern.

In the main there was silence between them. But when the first grey light of dawn was creeping over the sea, Tim ventured a question that had been perplexing him.

'Sink me if I understand why ye should be wanting to

go back to La Hacha. I thought as you was running away from it. Why else did ye ever consent to stop aboard when we weighed anchor?'

Blood laughed softly.

'Maybe it's as well ye should know. Ye'll be the better able to explain things to Mr. Fairfax in case they should not be altogether clear to him.

'Ye may find it hard to believe from what you know of me, but there's a streak of chivalry in my nature, a remnant from better days; for, indeed, it was that same chivalry that made me what I am. And ye're not to suppose that it's Fairfax I'm taking back to La Hacha and the vengeance of the house of Sotomayor. For I don't care a louse what may happen to the blackguard, and I'm not by nature a vindictive man.

'It's the little *hidalga* I'm concerned for. It's entirely on her account that we're going back, now that I've sounded the nasty depths of this fellow to whom in a blind evil hour she entrusted herself. We're going to restore her to her family, Tim, safe and undamaged, God be praised. It's little thanks I'm likely to get for it from her. But that may come later, when, with a riper knowledge of the world, she may have some glimpse of the hell from which I am delivering her.'

Here was something beyond Tim's understanding. He swore in his amazement. Also it placed in jeopardy, it seemed to him, the five thousand pieces he was promised.

'But if ye was running away from La Hacha, there must be danger for ye there. Are ye forgetting that?'

'Faith, I never yet knew a danger that could prevent me from doing what I'm set on. And I'm set on this.'

It persuaded Tim of that streak of chivalry of which Blood had boasted, a quality which the burly master of the *Heron* could not help regarding as a deplorable flaw in a character of so much rascally perfection.

Ahead the growing daylight showed the loom of the coastline. But seven bells had been made before they were rippling through the greenish water at the mouth of the harbour of Rio de La Hacha, with the sun already high abeam on the larboard side.

They ran in to find an anchorage, and from the poop-rail the now weary and blear-eyed Tim continued to be the mouthpiece of the tall man who clung to him like his shadow.

'Bid them let go.'

The order was issued, a rattle followed from the capstan, and the *Heron* came to anchor, within a quarter of a mile of the mole.

'Summon all hands to the waist.'

When the six men who composed the crew of the brig stood assembled there, Blood's next instructions followed.

'Bid them take the coaming from the main hatch.'

It was done at once.

'Now order them all down into the hold. Tell them they are to stow it for cargo to be taken aboard.'

It may have puzzled them, but there was no hesitation to obey, and as the last man disappeared into the darkness, Blood drew the master to the companion.

'You'll go and join them, Tim, if you please.'

There was a momentary rebellion.

'Sink me, Captain, can't you . . .'

'You'll go and join them,' Blood insisted. 'At once.'

Under the compulsion of that tone and of the eyes so blue and cold that looked with deadly menace into his own, Tim's resistance crumpled, and obediently he climbed down into the hold.

Captain Blood, following close upon his heels, instantly dragged the coaming over the hatchway again, and battened it down, insensible to the storm of howling from those he thus imprisoned in the bowels of the brig.

The noise they made aroused Mr. Fairfax from an exhausted slumber, on one side of the cabin, and Doña Isabel from a despondent listlessness, on the other.

Mr. Fairfax, realizing at once that they were at anchor, and puzzled to the point of uneasiness by the fact, wondering, indeed, whether he could have slept the round of the clock, got stiffly from his couch and staggered to the port. It happened to look out towards the open sea, so that all that he beheld was the green ruffled water and some boats at a little distance. Clearly, then, they were in harbour. But in what harbour? It was impossible that they could be in Cartagena? But if not in Cartagena, where the devil were they?

He was still asking himself this question when his attention was caught by sounds in the main cabin. He could hear the liquid voice of Alcatrace raised in alarmed, insistent protest.

'De orders, ma'am, are dat you not leabe de cabin. Cap'n's orders, ma'am.'

Doña Isabel, who from her port on the brig's other side had seen and recognized the mole of Rio de La Hacha, without understanding how they came there and without thought even to inquire, had flung in breathless excitement from her stateroom. The resolute Negro confronting her and arresting her intended flight almost turned her limp with the sickness of frustration.

'Please, Alcatrace. Please!' On an inspiration she snatched at the pearls in her hair, and tore them free. She held them out to him.

'I give you these, Alcatrace. Let me pass.'

What she would do when she had passed and even if she gained the deck, she did not stay to think. She was offering all that remained her to bribe a passage of the first obstacle.

The Negro's eyes gleamed covetously. But the fear of Fairfax, who might be awake and overhearing, was stronger than his greed. He closed his eyes, and shook his head.

'Cap'n's orders, ma'am,' he repeated.

She looked to right and left as a hunted thing will, seeking a way of escape, and her desperate eyes alighted on a brace of pistols on the buffet against the forward bulkhead of the cabin. It was enough. Moving so suddenly as to take him by surprise, she sprang for them, caught them up, and wheeled again to face him with one in each hand, whilst the pearls that had failed her rolled neglected across the cabin floor.

'Out of my way, Alcatrace!'

Before that formidable menace the Negro fell back in squealing alarm, and the lady swept out unhindered and made for the deck.

Out there, Blood was concluding his preparations for what was yet to do. Most of his anxiety about the immediate future was allayed by the sight of the broadbeamed Dutch ship that was to carry him back to Curaçao beating up into the roads, faithful to the engagement made with him.

But before he could think of boarding the Dutchman, he would take the eloping *hidalga* ashore, whether she liked it or not, and even if he had to employ force with her. So he went about his preparations. He disengaged the tow-rope of the longboat from its bollard, and warped the boat forward to the foot of the Jacob's-ladder. This done, he made for the gangway leading aft in quest of the lady in whose service the boat was to be employed. He was within a yard of the door when it was suddenly and violently flung open, and he found himself to his amazement confronted by Doña Isabel and her two pistols.

Waving these weapons at him, her voice strident, she addressed him much as she had addressed Alcatrace.

'Out of my way! Out of my way!'

Captain Blood in his time had faced weapons of every kind with imperturbable intrepidity. But he was to confess afterwards that a panic seized him before the threat of those pistols brandished by a woman's trembling hands. Spurred by it to nimbleness, he leapt aside, and flattened himself against a bulkhead, in promptest obedience.

He had been prepared for the utmost resistance to his kindly intentions for her; but not for a resistance expressed in so uncompromising and lethal a manner. It was the surprise of it that for a moment put him so utterly out of countenance. When he had recovered from it, he contrived to stand grimly calm before the quivering panic he now perceived in the lady with the pistols.

'Where is Tim?' she demanded. 'I want him! I must be taken ashore at once. At once!'

Blood loosed a breath of relief.

'Glory be! Have ye come to your senses, then, of your own accord? But maybe ye don't know where we are.'

'Oh, I know where I am. I know . . .' And there, abruptly, she broke off, staring round-eyed at this man, whose place and part aboard this ship were suddenly borne in upon her excited senses. His presence, confronting her now, served only to bewilder her. 'But you . . . You . . .' she faltered, breathless. 'You don't know. You are in great danger, sir.'

'I am that, ma'am, for ye will be wagging those pistols at me. Put them down. Put them down, ma'am, a God's name, before we have an accident.' As she obeyed him and lowered her hands, he caught her by the arm. 'Come on ashore with you, then, since that's where ye want to be going. Glory be! Ye're saving me a deal of trouble, for it was ashore I meant to take you whether ye wanted to go or not. Come on.'

But in her amazement she resisted, turning heavy to the suasion of his hand, demanding explanation.

'You meant to take me ashore, you say?'

'Why else do you suppose I brought you back to La Hacha? For it's by my contriving that we're back here this morning. They say the night brings counsel, but I hardly hoped that a night aboard this brig would bring you such excellent counsel as ye seem to have had.' And again impatiently he sought to hustle her forward.

'You brought me back? You? Captain Blood!'

That gave him pause. His grip of her arm relaxed. His eyes narrowed.

'Ye know that, do you? To be sure, he would tell you. Did the blackguard tell you at the same time that he meant to sell me?'

'That,' she said, 'is why I want to go ashore. That is why I thank God to be back in La Hacha.'

'I see. I see.' But his eyes were still grave. 'And when I've put you ashore, can I trust you to hold your tongue until I'm away again?'

There was angry reproach in her glance. She thrust forward her little pointed chin.

'You insult me, sir. Should I betray you? Can you think that?'

'I can't. But I'ld like to be sure.'

'I told you last night what I thought of you.'

'So ye did. And Heaven knows ye've cause to think better of me still this morning. Come away, then.'

He swept her across the deck, past the hatchway from which the angry sounds of the imprisoned men were still arising, to the Jacob's-ladder, and so down into the waiting longboat.

It was as well they had delayed no longer, for he had no sooner cast off than two faces looked down at them from the head of the ladder in the waist, one black, the other ghastly white in its pallor and terrible in the fury that convulsed it. Mr. Fairfax with the help of Alcatrace had staggered to the deck just as Blood and the lady reached the boat.

'Good-morning to you, Jorgito!' Blood hailed him. 'Doña Isabel is going ashore with me. But her brother and all the Sotomayors will be alongside presently, and devil a doubt but they'll bring the Alcalde with them. They'll be correcting the mistake I made last night when I saved your nasty life.'

'Oh, not that! I do not want that,' Doña Isabel appealed to him.

Blood laughed as he bent to his oars.

'D'ye suppose he'll wait? It'll quicken him in getting the coamings off the hatch, so as to get under way again. Though the Devil knows where he'll go now. Certainly not to Cartagena. It was the notion he took to go there persuaded me he was not the right kind of husband for your ladyship, and decided me to bring you back to your family.'

'That is what made me wish to return,' she said, her dark eyes very wistful. 'All night I prayed for a miracle, and behold my prayer is answered. By you.' She looked at him, a growing wonder in her vivid little face. 'I do not yet know how you did it.'

'Ah!' he said, and rested for a moment on his oars. He drew himself up and sat very erect on the thwart, his lean, intrepid face lighted by a smile half-humorous, half-complacent. 'I am Captain Blood.'

But before they reached the mole, her persistency had drawn a fuller explanation from him, and it brought a great tenderness to eyes that were aswim in tears.

He brought his boat through the swarm of craft with their noisy tenants to the sea-washed steps of the mole, and sprang out under the stare of curious questioning eyes, to hand her from the sternsheets.

Still holding that hand, he said: 'Ye'll forgive me if I don't tarry.'

'Yes, yes. Go. And God go with you.' But she did not yet release her clasp. She leaned nearer. 'Last night I thought you were sent by Heaven to save . . . that man. Today I know that you were sent to save me. Always I shall remember.'

The phrase must have lingered pleasantly in his memory, as we judge from the answer he presently returned to the greeting of the master of the Dutch brig. For with commendable prudence, remembering that Don Francisco de Villamarga was in La Hacha, he denied himself the satisfaction of such thanks as the family of Sotomayor might have been disposed to shower upon him, and pulled steadily away until he brought up against the bulging hull of that most opportunely punctual Dutchman.

Classens, the master, was in the waist to greet him when he climbed aboard.

'Ye're early astir, sir,' the smiling, rubicund Dutchman commended him.

'As becomes a messenger of Heaven,' was the cryptic answer, in which for long thereafter Mynheer Classens vainly sought the jest he supposed to be wrapped in it.

They were in the act of weighing anchor when the *Heron*, crowding canvas, went ripping past them out to sea, a disgruntled, raging, fearful *Heron* in full flight from the neighbourhood of the hawks. And in all this adventure that was Captain Blood's only regret.